CYNDI RAYE

A Tin Star for Christmas

THE BELLES OF WYOMING SERIES

A
Tin Star
for
Christmas

by

Cyndi Raye

---

1. http://www.CyndiRaye.com

The Creation of Belle, Wyoming

The story behind the missing bells of Belle, Wyoming.
On a wagon train to Oregon in the 1840's, Clara Brown's husband died of
Cholera, leaving her on her own. The wagon train did not allow single women
to travel alone, so she is ordered to leave.
She was rescued by a trapper and they fell deeply in love, creating their own
town not far from Ft. Bridger. They named the town Belle for the jingle bells
that were tied on her oxen when they first met. Now, years later, each Christmas
the tradition continues as the town places the bells on an ox or horse, gifting
rides to remember the legacy of the founders. The bells were safely put away and
only brought out each year for this purpose.
Except, this year, the bells have gone missing.
Are they ever found?

Chapter 1

"Sheriff, you busy?"

"Come on in, McKready. Shut the door behind you, we're not heatin' the outside!"

The telegraph operator hesitated for a split second before coming inside and dusting the snow from his shoulders. He stood in front of the huge wooden desk, holding out a slip of paper.

"Sheriff, you got a telegram from that, uh, young woman in Boston."

David Knight leaned forward, extending his hand over the desk. "Well, hand it over. What are you waiting on?"

McKready looked a bit sheepish, as if he didn't want to be standing in the sheriff's office. "Well, uh, it isn't the news you wanted to hear."

David pried the slip of paper from the man's hand. "I'll determine that for myself." The telegram was folded in half. He stood as he unfolded the paper, reading the news. A frown appeared on his handsome face, causing a small crease across his forehead. Dark hair fell over his brow, causing him to push it back with one hand.

Dear Sheriff Knight. Stop. I'm terribly sorry, I won't be arriving in two weeks. Stop. My father has been stricken ill. Stop. I won't be able to marry you after all. Stop. Good Luck to you. Stop. Miss Pearson.

He crumbled the note in his hand. A heavy, yet relieved sigh escaped. "McKready, don't you dare tell a soul about this telegram. I don't want anyone to know my intended bride is not coming."

"But, what about the Christmas Eve ceremony? You were planning to marry after getting to know each other. Thaddeus was holding a room for her at the hotel."

This time David ran a hand through his dark, thick hair. "I'll let him know he can cancel the room when the time comes. He never fills up, especially during the holidays. Keep this news under your hat."

McKready tapped his head. "I'm not wearing a hat!"

"You know what I mean. The last thing I want is a town filled with pitying stares."

"It's a darn shame about her jilting you. Why, your mother was looking forward to having a daughter. Now her Christmas Eve will be ruined as well."

"McKready, do not mention this to my mother, ever. Can I get your word?"

He nodded, a reluctant scowl on his face. "It's going to be hard to keep this quiet."

The sheriff leaned across his desk. He grabbed a handful of the front of McKready's shirt in his fist and glared, his soft brown eyes now dark and threatening. "I swear if you tell a soul, I'll find a reason to put you in jail over the holidays."

McKready laughed, although it sounded a bit nervous. "You can't do that! I've known you for ten years and consider you a friend."

"I can and I will! Give me time to figure things out. I don't want to disappoint my mother right now, either. Now, you promise me or I'll stick you behind bars and there will be no holiday celebrations for you!" The real reason he didn't want anyone to know was his own secret. He wasn't about to look like a fool in front of everyone in town. They were expecting their sheriff to marry on Christmas Eve. His mother had been bragging to everyone how her son was finally going to settle down.

Then there was his best friend.

Hope.

She appeared to be happy for him. Especially since she was planning on her own upcoming wedding in a few months. He had wanted to beat her to the altar. Then it wouldn't hurt so much when he watched her walk down the aisle.

The door swung open wide, gusts of cold air bursting through to cool the warmth from the pot-bellied stove. Chester Reynolds, the bank owner, popped his head around the door frame. "You better hurry, sheriff. The bells have been spotted!"

"Where?"

"Around the corner near the stables!"

David threw on his coat, not taking the time to button it. McKready followed behind as they crossed the street, treading the new snow that covered the ground. Snow was swirling around like tiny funnels and gusts, causing their view to be limited. David noticed his deputy standing in front of one of the water troughs, bent over, watching a figure as he made his way to where a horse was hitched in front of the livery.

A faint noise that sounded like bells jingling through the air caused David to turn towards the stranger. A dark hood hid someone's face. It didn't look like anyone from town. David knew everyone in Belle and this person was not at all familiar to him.

The figure in the hooded cloak was on his horse before David realized it. The sheriff hadn't put a hat on when he had left the office. Now, he regretted it, the wet snow splattering on his face blurring his vision even more.

The horse and rider began to ride down the street, away from town. This was their chance to catch the mysterious person who may have the Christmas bells. David realized if that cloaked figure had the bells after all this time, it was most likely a thief riding out of town. What else had been stolen? He had to take action.

The whole town was up in arms about the bells that had been missing for so long. "Deputy Will, if that noise I heard was what I think it was, we need to stop the bells from leaving here!"

He headed towards the younger man who had been given the job as deputy a week ago. At the last town meeting, the folks of Belle had voted to hire a deputy to help him. David had been the talk of the meeting as most of the women agreed that since he was getting married he'd need time to spend at home instead of working day and night.

At first, David thought it was a good idea, even if Belle, Wyoming was a relatively quiet town. Not much happened here on a daily basis. It was one of the reasons why he decided to come back when the town's sheriff had up and left a few years back.

David had his share of keeping order in wild cow towns with deadly gunslingers and rowdy saloons in the past. When his mother had sent him a telegram that they wanted a new sheriff they would be able to trust, he had handed in his badge and headed home to Belle, his days of lawlessness over.

He had missed home and was glad to be back.

He had especially missed his best friend.

No one knew the only reason he worked so late in the evening was because of Hope. She usually left the doctor's office to have supper at the café down the street. He'd usually catch up to her and they'd spend the evening meal together before he'd walk her back home. Even though she was engaged to be married, it was his duty as sheriff to make sure she got home safely since her intended was far away in Philadelphia.

At least that's what he told himself.

David had been thinking so intently about Hope he didn't realize the deputy had shouted to him. He shook the memories from his mind and tried to focus on what was happening. When Deputy Will drew the gun from his holster, David lunged forward to stop the young man, who was too quick to pull out his six-shooter. "Deputy, hold on before you go shoot-"

His words were cut off the moment David felt the jolt from the gun. The six-shooter misfired, the powder from the bullet exploding all around him and hitting David in the face. Startled, his world began to darken as a stabbing pain caused him to stumble back. David fell to his knees, connecting with the soft snow covering the ground.

"Sheriff, I'm sorry! I don't know what happened. Jesus, help us!" Deputy Will cried out to his Lord, his voice shaking so hard it sounded like his teeth chattered from the cold. David knew he'd caught the kickback from the powder right in his face. A cold fear began to hit him when he tried to blink, but his vision was so blurred all he saw were shadows.

"I can't see anything," he said, his voice low.

"I need some help!" Deputy Will called out to several townsfolk who peeked out of their place of business when the gun went off.

Shadowy figures ran towards him. David lifted his hands out in front of him, trying to keep others from getting too close. He didn't want anyone touching him, causing him to hurt more. The pain was excruciating now as he gasped in heavy, shuddering breaths. He felt a yank on both arms as his body was lifted up. His boots were dragging along the boarded walk, the heaviness trying to take him somewhere other than the present. He wanted to help them as he tried to lift a foot but it was no use.

"Doc Roberts is in! Run and get Miss Baker. Hurry!"

He was moving closer to the building, he knew that much. David tried to open his eyes but when he did, sparks of pain shot right through his eyelids causing even more anguish. He moaned. It hurt like the dickens. Through all the years of standing up to lawless men and criminals, David was disappointed he was going to go down from a misfired gun shot by his own deputy.

He was at peace if he didn't make it through. The years away had been hard, but he proved he was even tougher than most. Now, he was back home where he belonged. His mother's face swam before him in his mind's eye. She had been the force to get him back home, sending letters how she was praying for him to return to his roots. Now, he wanted to hug her and tell her how much those letters meant to him. David wanted to tell her how much he loved her, but it was probably too late.

He heard an angel's voice. He moaned again. A soft hand caressed his cheek. He leaned into it, trying to say her name. He blinked several times, forcing his eyelids to stay open. If he was going to die, he wanted Hope's face to be the last memory he'd have from this earth.

Chapter 2

HOPE'S HEART BEGAN to pound so loud when she realized who the man was that was being helped across the street. "Put him on the table," she ordered the men who were lugging the sheriff inside. She had touched his pale cheek, the coldness instilling fear like she'd never, ever felt before. There had been plenty of accidents, along with sickly people that had entered through these doors. When it came to David, well, he alone was her weakness.

It was the reason she was still here in Belle and not in the city of Philadelphia while her fiancé was attending medical school. He had wanted to marry her before he left but something had held her back from doing so. Sooner or later, after he was through his schooling and they married, she'd have to leave here and follow her husband wherever his new position as a doctor took him. A sadness the size of the tall pines in the distant mountains tore at her. This wasn't the way she had planned her life to be.

For right now, she had to clear her head and get David the help he needed. She filled a bowl with water and took out two clean towels from the shelf. The doctor's office was set up with the two front rooms used as his public offices, while the rest of the house was the doctor's own quarters. She loved the older man who kept the townsfolk safe and healthy. He was smart and tried to teach her how to nurse even though she'd never had proper schooling.

Smiling, she dabbed a towel in the cool water, placing it over David's forehead. He lifted his hand and she took it in her own, the coldness seeping into her warm skin. Hope leaned over him, her mouth close to his ear. "Hush, David, it's all right now. Everything will be fine."

He moaned, his fingers locking together with her own. At first he held her so tight she worried he'd cut off the blood circulation. As she whispered in his ear, his breathing became steady as his chest moved up and down. His fingers began to slowly relax.

"Good job, Miss Baker. Now, if you will step back, I'd like to take a look at the patient."

Doc Roberts was a tall, thin man who wore thick spectacles upon a rather enormous nose protruding from his face. He wore his hair longer than most men his age and it had long ago turned white.

She took a step back while trying to release her hand from David's own. Except his fingers had locked around hers once again. "I'm afraid the patient isn't letting go," she announced.

"Don't worry. I can examine him like this."

She stood by, her hand grasped within his while the doc carefully lifted both sets of eyelids. The moment he touched anywhere on David's face, the patient moaned and squeezed harder. She leaned as close as possible and tried to soothe him with words. Just like she'd do to any other patient.

Except this one made her heart pound so fast she absolutely knew anyone within a five mile radius would know she was in love with him.

Hope didn't want anyone to ever guess her heart's desire. It was a sin to marry one man and love another. Was she doomed?

Another hiss and moan escaped David's lips. "Where am I?" he asked, his voice cracked and weary. She knew him like no one else and he never complained. He had to be in tremendous agony.

"Perhaps we can give him something for his discomfort first," she offered up. She hated to see him hurting so.

The doc stepped back and nodded. "I can't see what's going on if he won't let me get near." She scurried away to the cabinet where they kept all the medicines as the doctor gave her instructions. While she measured out enough to keep David calm, she heard the doctor talking to his patient.

"You are in my office, son. It's Doc Roberts. Let Miss Hope give you something for your pain and we will get to the bottom of this." He motioned for her to step forward. She pressed the tincture between his lips. David swallowed and coughed, but she noticed he began to relax almost immediately.

After several more minutes the doctor began his exam. Hope stood by his side, ready to assist. She stared at David's handsome face, now scarred with gun powder burns. His dark features were that of a strong man, one who was sure of himself in everything he did. Not too much happened here in Belle, but Hope knew he had a past that involved guns and bad men. He had told her a few stories since he came back home.

She took his hand again, even though he hadn't reached out to her. They had known each other since childhood. Most everyone here knew they had a special friendship. She always told him they were best friends forever. He had always grinned and ran his fingers across her cheek.

The doc stood back, instructing Hope. "He'll need to keep his eyes covered for at least two weeks. I've cleaned most of the gun powder from his eyes, but one can never tell in these instances if it has helped."

Hope went to the bin where long strips of bandages were cut up for the purpose of wrapping a patient's wounds. She carried it back to the table and began to wrap David's head, careful not to touch any of the burns. When she was finished, she whispered to her mentor. "Is he able to see?"

The doc shook his head. "We can never tell. I've cleaned the wounds but it is imperative he keeps the bandages on while the eyes heal. I'm going to assign you to this difficult duty since I know of your special friendship. The sheriff is a stubborn man. He will not be happy when he wakes up to find he is in total darkness. I'll have Mabel ready the room across the hall where he will be under our care until the bandages come off in two weeks." The doc's office was set up for this purpose. The room they were in was like any other doctor's office, but the one across the hall was more like a parlor with a bed. The doc kept it set up for his patients who needed overnight, prolonged care.

Hope had taken a room upstairs, across from Mabel, his housekeeper. The living arrangement had been perfect for Hope when her parents had died and she moved to town. When she had taken the job as an assistant to the doctor he had insisted she move in to one of the empty rooms upstairs since the job came with board. He had moved Mabel from the room behind the kitchen to the room beside hers. Now, she'd be under the same roof as David. How was she going to be so close and yet stay far away from him? He was already causing her to have heart palpitations just being in the same space. She simply wouldn't allow these feelings to go on. Hope had to pretend she didn't care as much as she did.

The sad part was that she was betrothed to a man she didn't love.

And, David was going to marry a mail order bride on Christmas Eve.

She had to remain professional around him during this time. Even though they were best friends, she had to keep him at a distance.

Except all she wanted to do was hold him in her arms and tell him he'd be fine.

Hope was worried. David was not an idle man. He didn't like to be contained. How was he going to make it through the next few weeks like a blind man?

The doc answered her concerns before they even left her thoughts. "I am assigning you to his care for the next two weeks. You can work here when I need your assistance and Mabel can lend a hand. But, for the majority of your duties, your attention must be with our young sheriff, here. We have a responsibility to make sure this man's sight is restored again. Hopefully."

"What if he won't listen?"

"Do whatever it takes to make him listen and follow our instructions. I'll have a long talk with him but it's up to you to remain in his presence when you are not working. He needs constant care. A man who is not able to see can get cranky and mean. If that happens, call me and we will settle him down. We may even have to send for his mother."

"I probably should go tell her before Lucy does and worries the older woman to death." Lucy was the town gossip. Nothing slipped past her.

"He'll sleep for some time. Make sure Sadie knows he'll be well taken care of. Send the deputy in to me so I can inform him of the situation."

Hope left the office to find Deputy Will pacing back and forth on the front porch. When he saw Hope, his boots came to a stop. "How is he?"

The man was clearly guilt ridden. "Doc wants to speak to you."

She barely got a chance to finish her sentence before the deputy was gone. She turned and headed down the street to see David's mother.

At the end of the street, Hope turned the corner. The first house on the right held so many dear memories it made Hope smile. She remembered how the two of them sat on the front porch while their parents visited with each other. There were so many memories it overwhelmed Hope. She took a deep breath and knocked on the front door.

Hope waited patiently knowing Sadie was shuffling around, her slow ageing body ridden with what the doctor called weak bones. She used a cane to help her walk, but was determined to live on her own. The thought never occurred to Hope until now, but David's mother was as stubborn as him.

The door opened after a bit. Sadie popped her head out. When she saw Hope she opened the screen door. "Come in, girl. How are you?"

"Good morning, Sadie. Can we sit down?"

Sadie stood there, blocking her for a moment before opening the door wider to let Hope in. "There is something in the air. What's wrong?"

"Please, Sadie, sit down."

"I'm fine right where I stand."

Hope knew she wouldn't budge. She prepared herself in case Sadie weakened and lost her balance. "I have some news for you about David."

The old woman nodded. Her hair was still a dark brown, the same color of her sons except it's shiny luster had faded somewhat over the years. "What is wrong with David? You wouldn't be here if something hadn't happened? Is he hurt?"

Hope nodded, placing a hand on the woman's shoulder. "The deputy thought he spotted a man with the bells this morning. When David went to assist, the deputy took a shot at the mysterious man and his gun backfired. David has gun powder burns on his face."

His mother closed her eyes. When she opened them, Hope saw relief. "Thank my good Lord he is alive."

"He is alive, Sadie. But I'm here to tell you that he was injured. His eyes were blistered with gunpowder and he will have to keep them bandaged for two weeks while he recovers."

"I better sit down."

Hope took the older woman's arm while she made her way to the rocking chair by the window. Sadie was articulate. She knew without Hope having to mention it that his eyesight may be in jeopardy. "Why don't I make you some tea."

"That would be nice. Do you have time to have a cup with me?"

Hope nodded. "I will sit with you." While she heated the water, Hope tried to talk about the holidays. Every time she glanced to David's mother, the older woman had her hands clasped together in prayer. Hope stayed quiet then, giving her the privacy she needed.

When the tea was ready, she handed Sadie a cup and pulled a chair beside her. "I'm sorry to bring you such sad news, but I didn't want you to hear it from the town gossip."

"Thank you. I swear that woman must sneak around for the purpose of finding out everything first. If she shows up at my door, I won't answer."

Hope patted her shoulder. "You do what's best for you, Sadie. You have been like a mother to me, even before mine passed on."

Sadie reached out and patted Hope's cheek. "You are so sweet. I'm still hoping David changes his mind about this mail order bride ordeal and marries you instead, dear."

Hope wasn't expecting his mother's confession. This was the first time she had ever heard his mother speak this way. "I'm sorry, what?"

"Oh, you heard me, young lady. I have known all along how you feel about my son. I can still see, you know. My bones may be brittle but my eyes are fine."

"Have I been that transparent?" Worry began to claw at her like a fish flopping on the ground. She wondered now how many others suspected the same thing.

"Only to me, dear. You hide it well."

Relief shot through her. "I'm destined to marry Frank."

"No. It will never happen. When was the last time Frank wrote you a letter?"

"Well, it's been awhile. But, he is knee-high deep in his studies. Becoming a doctor is intense. I'm sure he doesn't have the time." She didn't want to say he had written only once, about a week after he got there.

"I see. If he were in love, he'd be committed to you. Let me ask you this. When David was working in Abilene, how often did he write home?"

Hope closed her eyes. "At least once a month."

"He would faithfully send me a letter, but he also enclosed one for you."

"He had promised to do so when he left. We are best friends."

The older woman grunted. "If you say so."

Hope stammered. "We are best friends."

"How often did he write to you when he was in Deadwood working as a lawman?"

Hope sighed. "Every month."

Sadie patted her knee and leaned closer. "He never forgot you no matter how busy he was. I heard the stories of these wild frontier towns. I'm sure a man of the law would not have much time to write home, either. Physicians, lawmen, they both have tense, important jobs to do. But, David always found time."

"He is a good son to you."

Sadie's shoulders shook so hard her tea cup rattled on the saucer. Was she laughing at Hope? "Sadie, what do you find so funny?"

"You, my dear. When will you see what I have all along?"

Hope sighed. "You're right. I'm a hopeless romantic, Sadie. I've loved David since forever. But, we took a vow years ago that we'd never ruin our friendship that way. Once, he kissed me and I made him promise never to try that again!"

"You were younger then. I remember." She smiled, looking at the small table where a photograph of her husband sat in an oval frame. "You two were on the porch looking at the stars while we were all inside visiting. David's father went to check on the two of you and found you both in an embrace. His father thought for sure the next day he'd have asked for your hand. But a week later, David had left town. It was the last time his father saw him." A sadness shadowed Sadie's face. Hope knew it was because she was thinking of her long departed husband.

They sat there for a long time. Hope had tried to push that memory from her mind. After David left, she had sulked for so long it had been hard to go on. Her parents were aware and encouraged her to let Frank court her. When her own parents had died in that wagon accident on the mountain slope, Hope realized too late she had made a rash decision when Frank asked for her hand in marriage. It was foolish to do so but she hadn't known how to get out of it. She didn't want to hurt him. Frank had been kind to her. He had helped her get through the tragedy of losing both parents.

David hadn't been there for her. She was sure he'd have been but he had been gone, making a life elsewhere. Later, when he gave up his job and moved back home to become sheriff, it was too late. She'd already promised herself to Frank.

A sadness crept up her skin like a snake slivering through tall grass. They would always be best friends. Nothing more. She stood. "I better get back. Doc Roberts has assigned me to care for David. He has opened his second room for the patient. I came by to make sure you knew he will be well cared for. I'll make sure of it, Sadie."

Sadie smiled. "Of course, you will. I'll have someone bring me to visit tomorrow. He needs to rest today."

When Hope left, she took her time going back. The memories of that kiss so long ago on Sadie's porch flooded her mind. She wondered how in the world she'd stand being in the same room alone with her patient for the next two weeks!

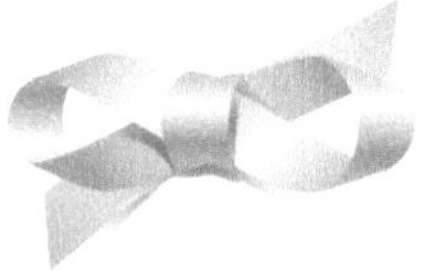

Chapter 3

David's eyes flickered open. His head throbbed. As he raised a hand to find out what was on his face, he felt the bandages around his eyes, reminding him of what had happened. The darkness was disturbing. He tried to pull the cloth away but his arm fell back, too weak to hold it up any longer. It took too much effort to try again so he laid still, in total darkness, contemplating what had happened.

He heard voices talking softly somewhere in the room. One of them stirred deep in his soul. "Hope?" he called out, his throat dry, reaching out his other hand until her familiar fingers fell into his own.

"I'm here, David." Her voice, like the sound of an angel, whispered in his ear.

He turned towards the sound. "It's dark."

"Doc Roberts has a bandage covering your eyes."

"I am aware. Tell him I'm awake. I want these off now."

He heard the sigh. She squeezed his fingers. "I'll be honest with you, David, the doctor is in with another patient right now, but he's not going to take off your bandages. You are stuck like this for two weeks."

He tried to sit up but his body was too weak. What had happened to him? She was still holding his hand, making him fully aware she was close by. It gave him peace of mind knowing she was here. Her other hand settled on his shoulder and she gently pushed him back. "Please, David, you need to rest. There's nothing that can be done right now."

"I can't stay still for two weeks. There's too much work to do. Who is going to run the show?"

Her soft laughter filled his ears. He leaned towards her voice. "David, it's for the best. If you don't leave the bandages on, your sight is at risk. Deputy Will is taking care of things. He said he'll give you a daily report once you are feeling better. Right now, you are stuck with me for two weeks."

He grinned. "That's not so bad."

She smiled even though he wasn't able to see. And yet, he knew she was smiling. "Doc Roberts has assigned me to be your nurse. In two weeks time, he'll remove the bandages. Hopefully by then your wounds will be healed enough."

She didn't say what he had been fearing all along. Knowing the reason the doctor was keeping his eyes bandaged made him realize how serious things were. What if he wasn't able to see? He'd have to give up his job as sheriff. He'd be worthless.

He'd be useless.

"Thanks for taking care of me, Hope. I'm glad it's you and not old Mabel. She can get cranky."

Hope giggled. "Now, you hush. She takes good care of all of us. She's no nonsense and the doctor likes her that way."

"The doc?" He grinned, the movement causing his face to hurt. The pain was still there, although it had settled down some. "Are you telling me the doc and Mabel have something going on?"

"I see our patient is awake?" The doctor's boisterous voice overrode anything Hope was about to say.

"Good morning, Doc. Guess I owe you a thank you for saving my life."

"Your life wasn't in danger, son. But, if you don't keep those bandages over your eyes, they will be in danger. There's a chance your eyesight may not return."

Hope squeezed his hand. "Time will tell," she told him.

"I must insist you hear the truth, son."

"I understand what's at risk. Why am I so weak?"

"The laudanum is keeping you quiet and causing the weakness. I'll be weaning you off of it over the next few days, but I'll warn you now, the burns will be painful."

That's all he needed, more pain. David was ready to resume his job. He didn't like to be idle. Somehow it made him feel like less of a man. "I'm not sure if I can sit around doing nothing for two weeks." His frustration gnawed through his soul.

"You won't have to. We'll get you up and about and Miss Hope will be with you. She is your eyes until the bandages come off." The doctor's voice got closer. He must've been leaning down to examine David's face. "Do you promise to keep your hands off those bandages, sheriff?"

The doctor was pretty slick. He knew David well. Now he'd have to make a promise and stick to it, even though he was itching to tear the strips from his eyes. "You have my word."

"Very good. Now, Miss Hope, I want you to cut his medicine in half. He'll need to rest as much as possible today and tomorrow we will get him up and into a chair."

"Yes, doctor." Hope let go of his hand and began to make noise from across the room. He knew the doctor was still there. David was surprised at how much more he was aware of without his sight. He was able to listen closely to what was going on around him, even aware of where each person stood in the room.

"I'll be back to check on you later this evening, sheriff. Until then, please heed everything Miss Hope tells you. Whatever she says, goes."

The door closed and all he heard were her footsteps getting closer. Before he was able to say a word, he knew she was standing over him. He smiled.

"What is the big smile for?" Hope ran a hand across his cheek to let him know she was there. He took a hold of her hand and kept it at his cheek, leaning in to her softness.

"I can tell when you are close by."

"Oh? How so?"

"I can feel you near me, or when you walk away."

She let out a sigh. "Can you tell I have some medicine for you. Open up."

He felt the edge of the glass at his mouth and opened up as the liquid trickled down his throat. He held onto her hand a few minutes longer before reluctantly letting go. "Thanks for everything, Hope. I'm sorry you have to be taken away from your duties to take care of me."

She ran a hand across his cheek. "It's not so bad."

He grinned before yawning, letting out a deep sigh. "Not for me."

Her body shifted and he knew she sat beside him, still holding his hand. "Not for me, either," she told him as the medicine began to take effect.

<> <>

David woke up, his groggy brain trying to focus.

"David, Deputy Will is here to see you. I'm going to step outside while he visits."

"I'm hungry."

"That's a good sign. I'll be back with some breakfast."

"Breakfast? How long have I been like this?"

"It's been one day."

David had felt her presence during the last few hours. Had she been sitting by his side all night long? "Did you get any sleep?"

"Some. I've slept on and off while you were snoring away."

David grinned. "I don't snore!"

Her laughter faded as she left the room.

He heard heavy breathing and knew the deputy was standing there, assessing him from a distance. "Get on with it, Deputy. What are you looking at?"

"I'm sorry, sheriff. I came to see how you were feeling?"

"I'm in pain. How do you think a man feels whose had his face burned with gun powder?"

He wanted the deputy to feel remorse for pulling out his six shooter before assessing the situation. Life as a lawman was a dangerous path. David needed his deputy to learn from this disaster.

"I'm sorry, sheriff. It was an accident."

David nodded. He knew it was but that didn't excuse the man. He was young and green. "If you are going to be working under me, deputy, there are some lessons here to be learned. That six shooter stays in your gun belt unless you are prepared to pull it out to kill a man."

"I just wanted to stop the rider from getting away."

"Deputy, what if someone, a child or a woman had been walking along the street when you shot blindly and been hit?"

The deputy took a shattering breath. "I've had nightmares about that all night long."

David tried hard not to feel anything. He had to be tough. "Deputy, I want a report each morning. In a few days, I'll have someone bring me over to the office to see how you are doing. The next two weeks are now a trial period for you. If you fail, your know what will happen."

When nothing was said, David cleared his throat.

"I'm sorry, I was nodding, Sheriff. I forgot you can't see. Oh, shoot! I didn't mean to say that!" He let out a rattled sigh.

David tried not to grin. He was honestly feeling some empathy for the deputy. "I am well aware of my state, deputy. Go on now, get back to work."

"Yes, sir. Have a good day. Er, well, have a better day than yesterday. I'll see you tomorrow," he said, his words all jumbled together.

David knew the moment he was gone. He shook his head, realizing the man had a long way to go to redeem himself. They'd work on that when David was feeling better.

The door opened. The sound of her shoes padding softly while she walked across the room made him smile. "Hope?"

"Yes, it's me. I brought you some breakfast."

"Will you have some with me?"

"I've already had mine. I'll help you."

He forgot he'd need help with eating. David ran a weak hand through his locks of thick hair. He listened while she set the tray down, then her warm hands were on his shoulder. He wanted to wrap his arms around her and pull her close. Dare he?

"I'm going to put a pillow behind you and help you to sit up. Lean forward, David."

He did as told and before he knew what was happening, he was sitting up in bed with a tray on his lap. He heard the legs of a chair scrape across the floor.

"Hope?"

"Open up, David."

He barely had a chance to say a word before she pushed a forkful of flapjacks in his mouth. Without being able to see, he savored the sweetness as warm syrup meshed with the cooked floury cake. He moaned, swallowed and opened his mouth again. "I'm starving," he told her.

She shovelled more in. "My goodness, chew the food!"

He leaned back against the pillow, his chin in the air, savoring the taste again. Not having his eyes to see made him so aware of the sense of taste.

He leaned his head front. "More."

She obliged, making short retorts as he cleaned the plate. She dabbed at his mouth, fussing with him about his manners. "You didn't even thank the good Lord before you ate," she accused.

"I did, too. He knows I'm grateful. Especially for you."

She ran her hand across his cheek again. "I hear a telegram came from your bride to be. When is she due to arrive?"

David heard a hesitancy in her voice he'd never have noticed before now. With his eyesight gone, he was so aware of the way she walked, talked and even her sigh was becoming a signal to him that something wasn't right in her world. Hope had been his best friend for a long, long time. They had shared every single day together when he had lived here before.

Ever since he came home they saw each other often. Even the evenings when they ate supper at the café together, it had been different for the two of them. He thought it had been because they were adults now and both were promised to someone else. But, now, he wasn't so sure. He knew what he felt deep inside for her. Some days he thought she felt the same way, like when she laid her hand gently across his cheek, looking him in the eye with a softness in hers it made him draw in his breath.

"David?"

He shook himself, realizing she was waiting for an answer. Now would be the perfect time to admit his mail order bride wasn't going to come after all. "I'm not sure."

She rattled a cup and felt the tray being removed from his bed. "You're not sure? How can that be? Mabel was sending a telegram to her sister when McKready had told her to hurry since he had a telegram to deliver to you from your bride to be in Boston."

He stilled. What in the world was he supposed to say? He didn't want Hope to know he got dumped, not now, not when she was so happy and waiting on her fiancé to return to marry her. He realized then that he'd be watching her get married before he did. That was exactly why he decided to get a mail order bride in the first place. He didn't think he'd be able to bear the sight of her marriage ceremony.

Or, was he being downright selfish?

He didn't want to watch her marry someone else! Now, it looked like he would have no choice. What made him think that if he had already gotten married, it would make things easier?

He was a fool.

He realized it now more than ever.

He should tell her right now.

God forgive him for the lie, but he wasn't ready to tell her yet.

"Her train was delayed a few days due to a relative becoming ill." Would that be enough to satisfy her?

Hope spoke up, too fast and too loud. "Oh? I hope it doesn't stall her for too long? We have a wedding on the eve of Christmas."

"You can stand in for her if you'd like."

Hope gasped. "David! What a strange thing to say. Why, what in the world would she say to that? You must be delusional. This medication is starting to harm you more than help. I need to speak with the doctor. I'll be back, sit back and relax."

David heard the door close as her feet scurried across the hallway. He knew the exact moment she went in to see the doctor. Each noise had a distinct sound, the location of a door closing or footsteps walking becoming more familiar to him.

He grinned. She almost flew out the door when he mentioned she could stand in for the non-existent bride. He was afraid that was the only way he was going to marry this year. Somehow, he didn't think Hope wanted that. Even though at times he felt like she wanted to be more than friends. Was it him? Or, did she truly care about him more than a best friend should? Without his eyesight he was becoming more and more aware of other's emotions and thoughts. How can that be?

Except he had to remember she was waiting on a man from Philadelphia to come home and marry her. It reminded David any chance he ever had with her had been over the day he had left town so many years ago. Once her fiancé came back and they married, she'd be gone from here, this place where they grew up together. Belle would not be the same without Hope.

How was he going to live here and work everyday without her? How would he get by without seeing her at least once a day?

He'd never hear her sweet voice again. He'd never see her beautiful face again. Her gentle hands would be touching someone else's cheek. He was so lost in his thoughts he never heard his mother enter the room until the scrap of a cane slide across the wooden floor. "Mother?"

"Son. How are you feeling?" She leaned down and kissed his cheek before taking a seat on the chair. He knew the exact moment her cane was laid across her lap.

"I'm good, Mother. You didn't have to come all this way to see me."

"Of course I did." She lifted her cane and tapped him on the arm. He laughed, pulling his shoulder back.

"Ouch!"

"Shh, not so loud. The doc will think I'm beating on you." Her voice was filled with mirth.

"I may tell him you are!" He looked her way and gave her a huge smile.

"Son, I wish you'd forget about marrying this mail order bride you sent for. She isn't the one for you." His mother had a way of coming right to the point of a conversation.

"What makes you think I haven't reconsidered?"

He felt her lean forward. Her voice was closer. "Have you now? Perhaps spending time with Hope will make you realize what is right in front of you is what you wanted all along."

David didn't acknowledge she may be right. He already figured that out. There was one problem and it was Hope's marriage to her future doctor. "Frank Wilson is going to be her husband when he returns from Philadelphia."

His mother hissed. "Don't be too sure of that, son. He hasn't written to her except for one time since he's been gone."

David's head came up off the pillow. "What? That's preposterous! Why in the world isn't he keeping in touch? I'm sure he's busy with his studies, but even so, he should be writing to her on a regular basis. Why hasn't she mentioned this?"

"It hasn't come up. I only found out yesterday when she came to tell me about your accident. Perhaps you need to find out what's going on."

David nodded. "Perhaps."

Chapter 4

When Hope realized David's mother was with him, she tried to stay away to give them privacy. Doc Roberts was on his last patient, an older woman who was talking the old doc's ear off. He didn't seem to mind, even encouraging her with questions. Instead of rushing the woman out the door, he interrupted her only once to let Hope know she was finished for the day and to take care of her patient in the adjoining room.

Right before she was about to enter into David's room, she heard his mother talking in hushed tones. Hope leaned her ear against the door to hear what they were saying. She didn't want to interrupt anything private.

In the back of her mind she saw her own mother's finger wagging back and forth and those wise words telling her not to impose on other people's conversations. Now, she realized her mother had been right because Sadie was telling David how Frank hadn't sent any letters since the first week he'd been gone to Philadelphia.

She hadn't wanted anyone to know.

Or, had she?

David's mother wanted the two of them together so Hope understood why she was telling him. Had she known his mother would say something?

Now David knew her fiancé hadn't even bothered to keep in touch.

As she made her way to the kitchen, she swore if David made any remarks about her current situation, she'd have a few things to say to him. Yet, as she washed up the dishes from breakfast, a smile splayed across her face. Maybe it was time Hope took charge of her life.

She was going to contact her fiancé once and for all. Even though she had sent many letters before, she always told him if he was too busy not to write back. Yet, she had longed to hear something from him. Today, after she made sure David was settled and comfortably resting, she'd go to the telegraph office and send her fiancé a heartfelt telegram.

Satisfied she'd made the right decision, she made her way back to her patient as Sadie was leaving. The older woman gave her a peck on the cheek. "Good-bye, dear. You're taking good care of my boy."

"Thank you, Sadie. Would you like me to walk you home?"

"No need." She patted the younger woman's hand. "Deputy Will is waiting outside to assist me home. He's had a complete turn around, helping others, knocking on doors to make sure some of the elderly are okay."

"Good for him. Maybe this accident has changed his demeanor."

"I believe so, and for the better." Sadie stepped out on the porch to find the deputy with his arm out to help her down the stairs. Hope was still smiling when she walked into David's room.

"What are you smiling about?" he asked.

She was surprised he was able to tell since he was unable to see. "How do you know I'm smiling?"

"Lucky guess. I figured if you weren't, it'd put a smile on your face anyway."

She went to the bed, pulling the blanket up over his waist. It had fallen down somewhat. He reached out and covered her hand with his. She stared at his face, watching as his mouth opened as if he were about to speak and then clamped shut.

Had he wanted to mention the fact her own fiancé didn't take the time to write her a letter? The more she thought about it from someone else's perspective, it was rude of her fiancé not to write, no matter that she had told him not to if he was too busy. He should have anyway. She was going to get to the bottom of things. Today.

"The doc wants me to cut your medicine in half." She placed the glass to his mouth as he took it in, dribbling a little down his chin. "This will make you sleep but for not as long. Soon, you won't need this to rest." She wiped his chin, admiring his strong features.

He nodded, his chest moving steadily while she stared at him. He was so quiet it worried her. "David? Is everything all right?"

He lifted her hand and placed a gentle kiss on the top of her skin. "It's more than all right."

"Your medicine will take effect in a few minutes. I'm going to run an errand and will be back before you wake up." She placed a small bell in the palm of his hand, closing his fingers around it. "If you wake up before I get back and need anything, shake the bell. Mabel will be here to help."

"Mabel?" His words sounded faint so she knew the laudanum was starting to take effect.

"Yes. Doc Roberts has gone fishing for a spell. He usually does on Thursday afternoons. I'll be right back. Rest now."

"Promise?"

She stopped in her tracks and spun back to the bed. "Of course, I promise. Why wouldn't I?"

He grinned. "I always wrote to you. I never stopped."

Hope pressed her lips together. "It doesn't make a difference, David. You are getting married in less than two weeks."

She left before any more words were said between them. Hurrying across the street, several people waved to her but she didn't want to stop and give anyone a report on how their sheriff was doing. That was up to the deputy, who needed to redeem himself for his terrible mistake.

She made her way inside the telegraph office, looking back once to make sure the nosey town gossip was nowhere in sight. Satisfied, she slipped through the door. Mr. McKready was behind the counter, a curious expression on his face. "How do you do, Miss Hope."

"Good afternoon, Mr. McKready. May I send a telegram, please?"

He handed her a slip of paper. "Certainly. Write your words on this and I'll send it right out."

She took the pencil and slip of paper, then moved down a bit, away from his curious eyes. She was sure he was wondering who she was trying to contact. He'd know soon enough. After several changes, she read it again, satisfied. "Here you go."

McKready pushed a pair of spectacles past the tip of his nose. A light crease ran across his brow as he leaned into the machine, tapping away. He looked up at her several times, a brow raised. She ignored him. It was none of his business and he had better keep it to himself.

She sighed. "How long does it take to reach the recipient?"

He lifted a finger for her to wait. When he finished, he handed the note back to her, along with the bill owed. She paid him and waited for his answer. They stood silent for a few minutes, then she heard a little buzz on his machine and he looked up and smiled.

"Done. Your telegram will reach it's destination in about four minutes. Now, the telegraph operator has to find your young Frank. I don't know how long that will take. Philadelphia is a rather large city from my understanding."

She nodded. "I'm not so sure he is mine any more."

"Oh?" McKready crossed his arms and ran a finger across his thin moustache.

She spoke out before realizing what she had said and knew he was waiting for an explanation, but didn't feel inclined to give him one. "You make sure no one knows I'm waiting on a telegram, promise me?"

"Sometimes this job isn't all it's cracked up to be."

Hope knew that if he promised, McKready would honor it. "Make sure that Lucy doesn't find out."

"That woman! I'd never tell her a thing. She'd have all kinds of rumors spread from here to California before you let the door slam shut!" Even though he said it, there was a softness in his voice when he spoke of the town gossip.

Hope left the telegraph office wondering if McKready and Lucy didn't have more in common than anyone knew.

There was an eerie chill in the air, more so than usual. The snow kept falling but that never bothered Hope. This cozy town nestled between snow covered mountains felt like home. She loved this time of year. People didn't seem so hurried even though Belle wasn't a busy town. Something magical happened during the holidays.

She wished something magical would happen to her. Hope stopped in the middle of the street. She looked up at the clouds that were forming, dulling the sun from shining down. It was a dreary day but even so, the townsfolk seemed to be content and happy. Yet, the air felt bitter cold, like a storm was brewing. Every year around this time it snowed but there was something in the air she wasn't sure about.

When she had walked into the telegraph office, she had been determined to end this farce of an engagement. She understood medical training was intense but if he cared about her, he'd have contacted her more often. It was time to let him go. She didn't love him and it wasn't fair to pretend any longer. Hope squared her shoulders. Once she heard back from Frank, she was going to tell her best friend the truth. It was a shame it took so long to get a letter to Frank, otherwise, she had to send a telegram to end a relationship. Or, a lack of a relationship.

Looking back, Frank had been the type of man that always came to the rescue. After her parents died, he stepped up to the plate, helping her get through a bad time. It was in his nature. She wasn't even sure why he asked her to marry him or why she even agreed.

Hope didn't want someone to rescue her. Frank had a giving heart and would do well as a doctor, but she didn't want to leave her home. She didn't care for him enough to do so. A pang of guilt sent ripples through her whole body.

She knew there was no hope for the two of them. She had always loved David. Even after he left, she had loved him still. Making a decision to marry Frank had been rash and unfair. When David came back to take the job as sheriff, he had looked so disappointed to find out she was already engaged.

She remembered the way he looked when he wished her well. He had been smiling, but now that she thought about everything that had happened, the smile had never reached his eyes. Frank would be done with his medical studies in the Spring, when the two were supposed to be wed. When David had found out, he had sent for a mail order bride and they were to be married Christmas eve. Before her marriage to Frank. He had never even mentioned wanting to get married. She had remembered him as saying he had no such desire. Then all of a sudden, when she had reminded him of her impending plans in the spring, he decided to get married out of the blue. With a woman he didn't know. On Christmas Eve of all times.

She turned away from the doctor's office, walking down the boarded walk, past the mercantile and bank. Hope needed to think. Awareness was coming to her like nothing she had ever before experienced. Everything the sheriff had done in the last year was a big sign he cared about her.

The walks home from the café every single night. He kept saying it was his duty since he was sheriff. He told her Frank would want him to make sure she was safe. Belle was one of the safest places in the territory. It was a safe haven because of him. David had a reputation of sorts. Everyone had heard the stories of how he had to arrest some hardened criminals and he knew how to keep order.

Those who knew David also knew he was one of the most gentle souls that lived. His mother was wishing for the two of them to be together and was upset he had sent for a mail order bride.

Where was his mail order bride? She was delayed, he had said.

She stood at the edge of town, staring at the livery.

Then she turned and marched right back to the telegraph office.

* * ⚕ * *

<><>

DAVID HAD AWAKENED several hours ago and she still wasn't by his side. Mabel had arranged his covers and grunted a few times. She had tried to tip-toe across his room but the moment he heard someone walking he knew the sound of Hope's shoes. "Who is there?"

She had grunted. "Mabel," she offered, although her voice was flat, devoid of any emotion.

David had tried to be cheerful but she was having none of it today. She wasn't happy her duties included taking care of a patient. He supposed he didn't blame her for being upset. "I'm sorry you have to check in with me. I'm fine though until Hope gets back. Have you seen her?"

"She went to run a few errands. What can I do for you, Sheriff Knight?"

"Smile."

"I beg your pardon?"

"I said smile."

"How would you know that I'm not smiling?" she questioned, her flat voice making it obvious to him there wasn't even a curve along her cheeks.

"You'd be amazed at the things you recognize without sight."

"I'm sure. Is there anything else?"

"No, ma'am. But, I will get you to smile yet."

He heard the distinct start of a chuckle before a tsk, tsk sound came from the room. "I'll close the door. Miss Hope will be back shortly. I believe I see her across the street."

David was anxious to see her. He decided that no matter what, he would tell her the truth about the mail order bride. Even though he knew she was getting married to someone else, she was his best friend. He had no right to keep something from her. Why he even tried to was beyond him. What had he been thinking?

Friendship came first. He loved Hope. With all his heart, he loved her enough to know that she deserved happiness. If Frank was the one she wanted to be with, then he wanted to be able to wish her well. Although, if Frank knew her and truly loved her, he'd have sent more than one letter. A heaviness weighted his chest at knowing in a few months she'd belong to another man.

The town would be anxious for a beautiful wedding for the doctor's nurse and then they'd wave goodbye as she left with a man who didn't even deserve her. David didn't want to think about losing her. But, he also didn't want her to leave his life without knowing the truth.

He had to make the best of things while they lasted. While he had Hope so close. He longed to see her face, to look into her beautiful eyes and taste her lips. Even though she had pushed him away so long ago, he had never forgotten that first kiss. He had remembered the promise. They'd always stay best friends. It was why he was going to be honest.

"Why the frown?" her soft voice reached him. He had been so intent thinking about her, his other senses never kicked in.

"I didn't hear you come in," he told her, turning towards her sweet voice.

"I tried to stay quiet. I thought you were fast asleep until I realized you were in deep thought."

"You know me so well. Come here." He held out his hand.

Her hand enveloped into his. They were a perfect match.

Chapter 5

Hope shivered. He took her hand in his, its warmth reminding her what it was like to be in his presence. David was a man who held nothing back. He had always been honest and kind to her.

"You wrote me every month while you were gone from here," she whispered, her voice emotional.

"You were my best friend. Still are, I hope." He lifted her hand in his and again pressed his mouth to her hand. Did best friends do this? A smile tugged at her cheeks. David had always been a different sort. He made his own way and on his own terms.

"Of course we are best friends. David?"

He looked at her even though he was unable to see. She felt him staring right through her. How was that possible?

Even though the doctor's house was built well, the shifting weather caused some branches from the tree to whack the side of the house, against the window pane. The sound startled them both.

Hope let go of his hand and went to the window. "It looks as if there is a bad storm rising," she told him. "Doc went ice fishing. I hope he hurries back."

"I can hear the wind howling, even through the thick walls," David mentioned. "Probably more so than usual."

Mabel knocked on the door, her hat and coat closed snugly. "I'm heading to the mercantile to pick up a few items in case we get snowed in. I'll be back shortly."

"Do you want me to come with you? It might be better if we go together."

"You hold down the fort here, Miss Hope. I'm fine. I hope Doc Roberts hurries back." A worried frown creased her forehead at the edge of her hat.

"I'm sure he left the moment the winds picked up. He knows how it can get at the drop of a thimble," Hope told her, trying to reassure the older woman. It was pretty clear Mabel had feelings for her employer.

"I can't see her face but her voice sounds worried," David mentioned as soon as the door closed. "I doubt this will be as bad as the blizzard we had last week. Most of the trappers are stuck up in the mountains, unable to get through the pass right now. Doc only went down to the stream right outside of town. He's nowhere near the pass."

"It is getting quite windy and the snow is blowing, making it hard to see."

"The doc will be fine. He's lived here all of his life and has been through these before. Where he goes to fish, there is an old cabin about twenty feet away, tucked against the mountain. He can hole up in there if he has to. We always make sure it is stocked with supplies. We can go get -"

His words halted when he realized he wasn't able to go anywhere.

"I'm sorry, David. I know what you were going to say."

Frustrated, he ran a hand through his hair. "This will be a great test for Deputy Will. He may have to go rescue the doc after the storm if he doesn't make it back in time."

She went back to stand at the side of his bed. Hope wanted to forget about the impending storm and get things over with. "I have to tell you something."

He nodded. "I have to tell you something, too."

"Would you like to go first?" she asked, her fingers fiddling with the corner of his blanket.

He shook his head. "No. Ladies first."

She smiled at that. He was always so kind. She took in a deep breath, drawing it out in slow motion. "I don't know how to tell you this, David, so I'm going to say it the best I am able. I adore you and don't ever want to lose our friendship. We've been best friends for so many years, I feel as if what I have done was deceitful in some way. To you and everyone involved."

He sat up a little straighter. "What did you do?" he questioned.

"This is quite difficult to say, so, here goes. I agreed to marry Frank because of feeling pressured after my parents died. I accepted his proposal out of some kind of duty. I thought I owed him."

"Hope. Are you telling me you don't love him?"

Why did he have to sound so cheerful? This was difficult as it was. His voice was quite exuberant. "I never loved him. I had strong affection for the man and was grateful that he was here to get me through one of my worst nightmares. After I moved to town and started working for Doc Roberts, I realized my feelings for him were not true. I was lying to myself and everyone else and I still allowed plans to be made for a spring wedding. A few hours ago, I sent him a telegram calling off the wedding and told him I'd send a letter explaining my decision. He sent a telegram back within the hour telling me I made the right decision. I believe he is glad."

She let out a deep sigh. It felt so good to say the words out loud.

He didn't move or say anything at first. The stillness in the room invaded her space and she realized as she spoke the words, her eyes had been closed the whole time. His even breathing was the only thing she heard in the room.

"Are your eyes opened or closed?" he asked.

That was an odd thing to ask, she thought to herself, but answered anyway. "Closed."

"Don't open them."

"All right."

"What do you see?"

"Darkness." She was so confused by his reaction. It wasn't what she had expected. "I just told you about my darkest secret and you want me to keep my eyes closed."

He reached over and took her hand, connecting on the first try. She felt his warm hand encase her own. "It's funny how we can see from our mind's view. Imagine, if you will, the wedding you had planned, but with someone else."

There was only one man she could imagine standing beside her. "Okay, I can see me standing at the altar."

"Imagine it isn't next Spring but Christmas eve."

"In two weeks, why that's impossible!"

"Just let your mind wander and imagine walking down the isle in a beautiful wedding gown."

"The doc at my side to give me away," she whispered, catching the excitement in the air. "He's been more like a father to me since my own passed away." Hope smiled. She imagined beautiful vases filled with flowers and a candle lit room. All the townsfolk watched as she married her best friend.

A gasp erupted from her throat.

"What is it? Tell me what you saw?"

Hope opened her eyes. David was looking her way, as if expecting her to answer. She'd never tell him that she saw him waiting for her at the altar.

Because he was supposed to be marrying his mail order bride on the very day she imagined herself standing there. But in her mind's eye, she saw David standing there, waiting for her.

The picture in her head was so real, it made her stomach quiver and her mind reel. She dropped David's hand and stepped back. She had to stop this silliness. It would never happen because he was to wed someone else.

"Hope? What did you see? Tell me?"

She swallowed. "I saw, um - "

A branch cracked against the side of the house, startling Hope. She jumped and cried out.

The cold air burst through the house as the front door opened and a figure slammed the heavy oak door shut. "Hello?"

It was Deputy Will. "We're in here!"

He entered the room, pulling off a pair of snowy gloves. "Miss Hope. If you don't mind, I have some private business to speak to the sheriff about."

He had entered the room at the perfect time. It saved her from explaining to David exactly what she had seen. "I'll go start on supper."

"I would cook for yourself and the sheriff, ma'am. Mabel headed out to the lake to check on the doc. I warned her against it but she insisted. I'm pretty sure both of them are holed up in the shack by now. Here is a bag of supplies she sent along."

As Hope made her way to the kitchen, she heard the two men talking business. The deputy gave David a report on the town. She turned the corner, trying to force her mind to think of something other than that startling image of the two of them standing in the church.

David had caused her to dream about things that would never happen.

He was going to marry in the same church on the same day as in her vision.

But it wasn't going to be to her.

A stranger was coming to town to take his hand and make him her husband.

A tear slipped down her cheek. Hope was not able to hold it back any longer.

The man she loved, truly loved, was going to be someone else's husband.

An hour ago she was pretty sure she had figured out that he had cared more about her than she gave him credit for. It had all pointed to the fact David was as much in love with her as she was with him. Then reality shook her to the very core.

How was she going to stand it?

At least David was right. The mind is so strong it made her imagine the two of them together, starting a life of bliss. She almost believed it was truly going to happen. Then he had her close her eyes and realize it would not be her but another bride standing next to him.

What a dose of reality!

At least she told him the truth about her situation. That was a weight off of her mind at last. If anything good came of this day it was that she no longer felt the pressure of marrying a man she never loved.

Tonight, she'd sit down and pen a letter to him, explaining why she chose to end their farce of a relationship.

A hour later supper was almost done. She heard a commotion in the parlor and went to investigate. Deputy Will was holding David up as the man leaned against him, taking a step towards the chair near the fireplace. Hope hurried to his side, taking his arm and guiding him to the chair. She ran for a blanket and tucked it neatly over his lap.

David leaned back and grinned. "I've been wanting to get up and about all day. Thank you both."

"I best be going now," the deputy mentioned. Once the wind stops blowing and daylight comes around, I'll take a sleigh and head to the cabin for the doctor. He's not going anywhere any more this evening."

"I'll expect a report in the morning before you head out. You'll have to stay at the sheriff's office in case someone is in need of help."

The cool draft disappeared a few minutes after the deputy closed the front door. Hope went over to the fireplace, adding more wood. She wiped her hands and sat across from David on a wooden rocker. "Are you comfortable?"

"Yes."

"Are you warm enough? I've stoked the flames."

"Yes." He leaned his head back.

"It's past time for your medicine."

"I can do without."

"Are you sure?"

"I'm sure."

Hope twiddled her fingers. She rocked back and forth. Were they going to continue the conversation from earlier? "Can I get you anything?"

"Hmm," he mouthed.

"David? Are you falling asleep sitting up?"

"Hmm," he said again. His chest rose and she was certain he had fallen asleep. She sat for awhile, staring at his profile, wondering what it would be like to, no! She had to stop thinking absurd thoughts. He was going to marry another woman. Someone who was about to embark on their town any time now. What if she wasn't able to get through the pass?

The thought made her heart race.

It was most certain the stage coaches had halted during this bad period of weather. Most railroads were shut down until the blizzard cleared up. No one would be able to make it here unless they had a few days of decent weather.

She turned towards the window. By the looks of things, this kind of storm might stick around for awhile.

Her thoughts went to David. He cared about her a lot. She knew it more than anything. Yet, he had sent away for a bride. Had it been because she had so stupidly taken the first offer of marriage presented to her instead of waiting to see if their relationship became more serious than a friendship?

"What are you thinking about?" His voice almost made her jump straight out of the rocker.

"I thought you were sleeping." Her voice shook and she gripped the sides of the wooden rocker.

"I wasn't. Our earlier conversation got interrupted. I've a feeling you don't want to continue it."

She shrugged even though she knew he wasn't able to see it. "There's no point. You're bride may arrive any day now, David. The only bride set to get married on Christmas eve is her."

"Are you certain?" he asked, his voice low, his jaw stiff.

Why was he continuing this farce? "You need to stop this nonsense, David. I'm not going to marry Frank. Not now, not ever.

Now, would you like to sit at a table to eat dinner or do you want me to bring you a plate?"

"It's nice right here. Would you mind?"

"Of course not. If you'll excuse me, I'll be back shortly." She left him sitting in front of the fire and busied herself in the kitchen. He was speaking strange things this evening. Had the blast of the gun made his brain mushy? He sure was acting strange!

<> <>

David smiled. He had to stop playing around and tell her there was no bride coming. He had wanted her to imagine the two of them getting married on Christmas eve but she wouldn't tell him what she saw in her imaginings. He was hoping to surprise her and ask for her hand now that her fiancé was out of the picture. Except there was something he needed to know before he asked for her hand.

While she was preparing the meal, David let the cover fall from his lap. He stood up and walked towards the fireplace, moving one foot at a time. He remembered there was a mirror on the wall right above the fireplace. The heat drew him to the center, where he stood facing the great wall. David slowly pulled his bandages down. The air in the room blasted his eyes, making them sting.

He blinked. Once. He knew he was standing in front of the mirror. The shadows that stared back at him were like a smack in the head. He had been denying there was a chance he would be blind. Now, he knew better. His vision was not returning. He covered his eyes back up, moving the bandages until they completely covered his eyes.

He stood still, his shoulders drooping, the heat from the fire so close he didn't care if it caught him on fire and burned him up. How was he going to survive as a blind man?

He'd have to give up his job as sheriff.

Hope.

He wanted to ask her to marry him, but not now. Not if he was unable to see.

What woman would want a blind man?

No one.

He was destined to live a life alone, in darkness. What was the point of living?

Hope stepped in the room. "What are you doing?" she called out. The rattling noise sounded as if she set down a plate. He felt her hand on his shoulder and arm. "Let me help you sit down, David."

After she got him settled in, she handed him a plate of food. Putting the fork in his hand, she helped him guide the food to his mouth. It was good but tasted like leather. He had no appetite today. Not after what he learned about himself.

"You are unusually quiet this evening."

He sighed. "I'm not hungry. You go ahead and eat."

"Are you certain?"

"Yes."

"Sometimes the medication will curb the appetite."

"I haven't taken any medication today."

She nodded. He knew it but he wasn't able to see it. Was this how he'd spend the rest of his life? If so, God had played a cruel joke on him.

"You seem uptight. Why don't I give you a small dose? It will help you settle in tonight."

He wanted to shake a fist in the air but held himself back. Anger, betrayal and trusting a force he had never seen engulfed his thoughts. He was unable to focus. Instead, he nodded for the laudanum. If he took it, he'd forget that he was blind as a bat.

First, he had to tell her about the mail order bride. She was his best friend and he wasn't going to lie to her any more. He at least owed her the truth.

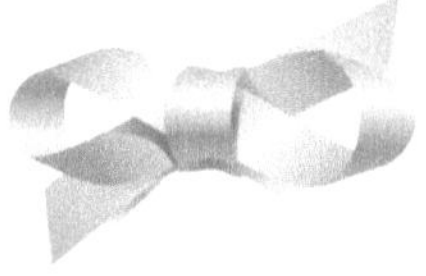

Chapter 6

Hope knew something was terribly wrong. They had been friends way too long not to see the signs. Something that happened while the deputy was here that was upsetting him. "Stand up, now, David. Let's go back to your bed and I'll give you a dose of medicine."

She led him to his bed, tucking the covers around him. The wind howled louder, making it feel colder than it actually was. His shoulders drooped more so than usual. She went to the small cabinet that held his medicine and began to pour out a smaller than usual dose. It was enough for him to be comfortable.

When she got to his bedside, he was staring at the window, where the wind was still roaring loudly. "I have something to tell you," he said, his voice so low she became concerned.

"Here, take this first, then we'll talk."

He shook his head. "You need to know there is no mail order bride coming, Hope."

She almost dropped the laudanum. "What?" Her voice was but a whisper. "She is delayed, I'm sure. When the pass opens she'll be here. David, why are you shaking your head?"

She sat down on the edge of the bed since her knees were starting to weaken. What was he saying?

She broke off her marriage to Frank and now this? She needed to know more. Excitement shot through her veins like a dose of laudanum to a sick man.

David continued to stare at the window, even though she was so close. "I got a telegram the other day. Her father is ill and she decided to call off the marriage and stay in Boston. I told McKready if he spills the beans to anyone, I'd throw him in jail."

Now she understood why the telegraph operator had acted so strange when she asked him if David had gotten any telegrams from his mail order bride. He had made a promise to David to keep it quiet. How hard it must've been for McKready.

A smile escaped her lips. "It's not so bad, David. I'm in the same position, giving up Frank. I guess you can say we both have been set free!"

"At least you're free to marry someone else."

She laid a hand over his without any response. Usually, he'd pull her hand to his chest or kiss her skin. Now, there was no reaction. "David. I'm not going to marry someone else. Why do you say that? You can marry anyone of your choosing now?"

She hoped it would be her, but his next words took any hope she had of the two of them away.

"I'll never allow myself to be a burden to anyone. No one wants a blind man."

She squeezed his hand. "David, don't be so hard on yourself. You don't know what you'll find when you take off those bandages. You still have over a week to go. Give yourself time to heal."

"I already know. I checked in the mirror earlier when you were making supper."

Now she understood why he had been standing so close to the fireplace. "You were told not to do that, David. The doctor warned you that if you take the bandages off too soon, your eyes may not heal."

He shrugged, the life drained from his body. She was well aware of his anger right now. Not knowing if you are able to ever see again must come at a pretty high cost. "Listen to me, please. It's too early to tell. You need at least another week to heal and know for certain."

He pulled his hand away from hers and sat back against his pillows. "There's no point in anything if I can't see. Go on Hope, get yourself married to a man worthy of you. I wish you well."

She placed the glass at his mouth and he took the medicine. Hopefully, he'd calm down and feel better once he slept. "Let's not talk about this right now, David."

"There's no point ever discussing this again. I'm finished, Hope. My life is over. I was going to ask - "

"You were going to ask me something?"

"Never mind," he murmured. The laudanum was starting to take effect. He relaxed his body and she stayed with him until he fell asleep.

The man was feeling all kinds of things right now. Denial and anger that he wasn't able to see yet. But, she was right. He needed more time.

What if David did lose his sight?

Then she would be his eyes. She'd teach him how to live without seeing.

She'd never leave him and she was going to tell him so.

They had a chance now to be together.

He was resting now, his face serene and peaceful.

She pressed her mouth to his forehead. "I'm not giving up on you," she whispered. "I'll never give up on you, David."

<> <>

McKready knocked on the door at first light. When Hope answered the door, the whiteness blinded her. The wind had blown the snow all over the street. It was hard to see across the road. Thankfully, it was much calmer than last night even though it still snowed.

"Come in, quickly." She pushed the door closed when McKready came inside. He shook his coat and stomped snow from his boots onto the foyer floor.

"Good morning, Miss Hope. I'm assuming our dear sheriff is up this morning?"

"He's actually not awake yet. Would you care for a cup of coffee?"

He shrugged off his coat, hanging it on the coat rack in the corner beside the door. "A cup of coffee sounds wonderful. I came by to check on David."

She led him to the parlor and poured them both a cup of hot coffee. Handing him a cup, she sat down in the rocker. "David was not a good patient yesterday. He stood here in this room and pulled his bandages down. He still can't see and he's terribly upset."

The telegraph operator nodded. "I had this urge to visit today. Perhaps we are more like brothers than friends. I felt as if something was off."

"Oh? Then, what do you have there in your pocket?"

McKready covered his front pocket. "It's um," His shoulders sagged. "It's another telegram from his mail order bride. She is waiting for a reply."

"Oh? He never replied? Oh, dear!"

McKready nodded. "She needs a reply back today."

It was time he knew she was aware of the truth of the matter. "McKready, David told me of her situation."

"You know? Does anyone else know?"

She shook her head. "No one. For now, let's keep it that way. There *will* be a wedding on Christmas eve."

A huge smile crossed the man's face, understanding what she was trying to say without saying it. "I hope so. I've been hoping so for a long, long time."

"You make sure David sends a telegram back to Boston today. Do I have your word?"

He nodded. "Yes, of course I'll make sure he agrees to it. She said if he doesn't answer, she will be obliged to honor his proposal even though her father is gravely ill and she doesn't want to leave him."

"Oh my! We can't have that, now, can we?"

Hope stood. She wanted to start making arrangements as soon as the storm subsided. "I believe it's safe to go in to see David now."

As McKready went to visit with the sheriff, Hope began to make a list of all the plans for Christmas Eve. She knew David was depressed and not himself but she also knew he wanted to marry her.

He almost spoke the words before he had checked his eyesight. Blind or not, she would be there for him.

She just had to make him understand she wasn't going anywhere.

<> <>

. . ⚘ . .

DAVID WOKE UP TO THE sound of someone breathing heavily over him. He listened for a few more minutes before his hand twitched. "McKready, is that you?"

"How did you know? I tried to stay quiet until you stirred."

David chuckled. "You were breathing over top of me. You didn't know that you make a grunting sound when you are concentrating, did you?" Every time McKready was sending a telegram he'd do the same thing, make the same type of noises.

McKready drew in a deep breath. "I don't do that!"

"You do, it's not noticeable to many others. Just to me. All my other senses are extremely accurate. I can tell if Hope is coming in the room or if it's the old woman, Mabel. Even the doc's footsteps are distinct. What do you want, McKready?"

"I hate to be the bearer of bad news, but you have an issue to take care of."

David shrugged. He didn't much care to take care of anything right now. The darkness made him feel as if there was nothing important enough to live for. He wasn't a person to give up too easily, but knowing he may have to live in this darkness the rest of his life was enough to make him feel worthless. "There's not much I can do as a blind man."

"Who says you're blind? Give yourself some time to heal, sheriff? You know what the doc said."

"Doctors don't know everything. The doc didn't see what I did, or rather, didn't see!" Bitterness spewed from his mouth. He tried hard to shake the resentment, but it hung over him like a dark cloud waiting to burst open and shower a horrendous storm below.

"You can be angry all you want, but if you don't respond to this telegram, you'll have a mail order bride on your doorstep in a few days."

"How so? I thought that was over and done with?" David turned his head, listening to the light footsteps outside his door. Hope was listening in. Even though he was upset, knowing she cared enough to listen to the conversation almost made him grin.

He shook himself. David had to stop caring about what she thought or how she felt. There was no hope for the two of them. Not as long as he was a blind man.

McKready was too quiet. "McKready?"

"Sorry, sheriff. I was shaking my head. Forgot you can't see! Oh, for Pete's sake, I'm sorry! I didn't mean to say that!"

"It's not like it isn't true. I'm a blind man, McKready. You may as well let everyone know."

"I'll do no such thing. Why, when Doc Roberts comes back today and hears you've been talking like that, you're lucky he don't keep you in bandages for another week after what you did last night."

"How do you know what I did? Were you talking to Hope?"

"I had a cup of coffee with her and she told me how badly you behaved. Shame on you, sheriff. You are supposed to be an inspiration to all those who are put in your path. How in the world can you be if you are feeling sorry for yourself?"

David restrained himself from lashing out at his friend. "It ain't none of your business, McKready. Go on, get out of here and do what you do best, send telegrams!"

"How do you want me to respond to your mail order bride?" McKready obviously wasn't threatened by his harsh words. David reminded himself they had known each other for a long time. There wasn't much the two couldn't say to each other.

"Tell her I'm a blind man and she best not come. Tell her to take care of her dying father."

"I'll tell her the last half. You don't know if the first half is true."

"May as well be. What's another week going to do? Nothing."

McKready's footsteps began to fade away. David knew when he got as far as the door, then his footsteps ceased. "You know, Sheriff,

I thought you were much tougher than this. Even if you can never see again, you have a lot of gifts to offer this town. It's a darn shame you don't see them, because I do. So does everyone else."

"Get out!" David sucked in air, trying to force himself to breathe. He didn't want to face the town at this point. Not now, not ever.

The moment the door closed, his senses perked up and he heard the two whispering in the foyer. McKready's voice was much louder than Hope's, but he knew they were planning something. How he knew was instinct. He'd been a lawman for too long. When people were trying to be sneaky he always seemed to know.

David didn't care what they were planning as long as it didn't involve him!

A shuffling sound alerted David that someone else was coming up the steps of the front door. A loud banging and a cool breeze fluttered across his room.

More talking and he heard the distinct voice of his deputy. A few moments later, the man entered his room, the cold from outside penetrating his nice, warm space. "Deputy Will. What's wrong?"

"Good morning, Sheriff. We have a problem. There is a large tree across the road towards the small lake where the doc is taking refuge. I climbed over it and hiked to the cabin, which isn't too far from there. I was going to help him get back here, but he insists he isn't leaving his horse and buggy behind. He won't be able to get them through. He said if the horse has to stay behind, he does, too. He said as long as no one needs medical attention, there is no reason for him to hurry back. Mabel insisted she had better stay there, too."

David didn't want to care. He shrugged at first. "What can I do? Nothing."

He heard the grating sound as the deputy rubbed his hands together to warm them up. "Most of the townsfolk will work together to help saw the tree up so we can clear the road. The stage may eventually come through now that the storm is dying down."

"How long do you suspect it will take?"

"A day, maybe two at the most. We have lots of help."

"You are the sheriff, do what ever you need to get the job done. You don't have to ask me for every little problem that comes along."

"Sir? I'm not the sheriff. You are."

David grumbled under his breath. "Right now, for the time being, you are in charge, Deputy Will. Use your own judgement. Mine is hampered right now. A blind man can't make decisions."

Deputy Wills left soon after. David was harsh with him this morning, but the man had to take charge. The town was going to have to make a decision anyway as soon as they learned he was as blind as a bat.

Hope tip-toed around the room but David knew she was there. He wasn't going to let her know just yet. He didn't want to talk to anyone.

Was he ever going to get out from under this heavy darkness he felt himself slipping into?

Chapter 7

"It's time for breakfast."

"I'm not hungry."

"Now, David. If you don't eat, I'm afraid I'll have to inform your mother how horribly you are behaving. I know how much you respect her and don't want her to worry about you. I'm sure you don't want her to concern herself as she sits all alone in her house during this winter storm, do you?"

"You're trying to make me feel bad. Stop that!" He grumbled more words under his breath. No matter what he said, Hope wasn't going to allow him to wallow in self pity.

She set the tray on his lap. "I would never try to deliberately make you feel bad, David. You seem to be doing that to yourself without my help."

"What's that supposed to mean?"

"Open wide," she ordered, shoving a forkful of freshly made eggs in his mouth before he was able to say anything else.

He chewed heartily before swallowing. "These are quite good."

"Thank you. You best eat. You need your strength."

A frown appeared. "I realized I am not able to check on my mother, now that you mentioned her and the storm all in one sentence." Hope realized too late how he was affected by not being able to just get up and do the things he always had.

"Don't worry, David. I plan to get you up and out of bed this morning. Then, when you are quite settled in the chair by the fireplace, I'll run to your mother's house and check on her."

David lifted his hand as if he were going to touch her. Hope held her breath, knowing if he did, it would be a good sign he was coming out of his bad mood. Then, he let his arm drop to his side.

Hope sighed in frustration. She wouldn't give up. Not on him. Not for anyone or anything. She wanted her David back.

Her mother hadn't named her Hope for nothing. She was going to give this man all of her hopes and dreams and wait for him to wake up to the fact that with or without sight, he was loved and fully capable of loving her back.

This was the season for love and hope. And miracles. He deserved happiness.

She lifted her head to the ceiling, looking up as if God were standing right there watching her. *Please, Lord, give me all your strength and courage to make David see what we all see in him. He is a good man. Help him to see with his eyes as well as his mind. Thank you, Lord, for all we have, amen.*

"What are you doing? Praying?"

She smiled. "You don't need your sight to know what I'm doing it seems. You've always been able to read me quite well."

"Every time I try not to think about my inability to see, you somehow talk about it as if it is a normal part of life. Don't you see, Hope, I'm no longer normal."

She read the frustration in his voice, but it wasn't going to deter her one bit. "Oh, I think you are normal." She laid a hand on his arm. "And quite the handsome man, too."

He turned away as if that would keep her from speaking more words. She leaned in and whispered. "I'm not going anywhere, David. You can grumble all you want. I'm here to stay."

He huffed. "When Doc Roberts gets back I'll ask him to put Mabel in charge instead of you. Then you won't have to worry about me any longer."

Hope giggled.

"What's so funny?"

"You'd last one day with Mabel, maybe two at the most, before you'd be pulling hair out of that fine head of yours."

She deliberately gave him a compliment. He needed to hear positive things about himself. She was going to build him up until he was bursting at the seams. The spirit of happiness fell over Hope in a way she didn't quite understand. Well, she was done questioning things for now.

There was a purpose for her to be taking care of David.

She wasn't going to deny she loved him, always had.

Now to get him to admit he still loved her and always had.

Perhaps she did need his mother's help in this situation.

She glanced at the clock on the mantel as she went to clean up the dishes. It was mid-morning. Hope quickly cleaned up her mess and helped David to the chair in front of the fireplace. "Are you going to sit still today and not try to look in the mirror again?"

He nodded. "You can take down that mirror. I'll never need it again."

Hope patted his shoulders and gave him a kiss on the cheek, making sure she ignored any negative comments he made. She was going to be so positive he'd want to be up and moving before he realized what had hit him!

"I'll be back with news of how your mother is doing. Stay here and enjoy the warmth of the fire."

She buttoned her coat and wrapped a scarf around her neck, pulling it across her chin and mouth. It was blistery cold out today.

Leaving the doctor's office, Hope pulled her wool hat down over her head, covering her ears better. She shivered as the cold seeped into her skin as she made her way down the street and around the corner.

She stood on the front porch waiting on David's mother to make the slow trek to the front door, she thought about the future. The future David was going to be a part of, even if he was denying it right now. There was nothing stopping the two of them from making a life together except for the man's stubborn pride.

The lock wiggled and the door swung open. "Hello, Hope. Come in and warm up."

Hope made some tea and handed a cup to David's mother. The more she thought about things, she decided his mother may be able to help get David out of his sad state of mind. "David is quite upset right now, Sadie."

"Why is he upset? Because of his injury?"

She nodded. "I'm afraid so. He lifted his bandages ahead of time, seeing only shadows and thinks he'll never be able to see again. Doc Roberts wanted him to wait a full two weeks and I'm afraid he jumped the gun and didn't listen."

The older woman smiled. "That sounds like my David." She leaned front. "He's quite naughty, isn't he? Just like his father was."

Hope watched as the older woman fixed her gaze on her tea cup, thinking of another place and time. It was plain to see she missed her husband dearly.

"How did you manage to keep him in line?" Hope wondered out loud.

A sweet smile spread across Sadie's face. "Oh, I never tried to. I loved him just the way he was, naughty or nice. He was my husband and my dear friend. We loved each other in spite of our faults."

"That's what I'm trying to make David understand. It doesn't matter if he doesn't have sight. I'll stand by him no matter what happens. I do love him, Sadie. He's been my whole life for so long I can't remember him not being in my thoughts for even one day."

A tear slid down Hope's cheek.

"Now, now, dear. David will come around. What about his mail order bride? Did he send her away?"

Hope smiled through her tears. She wiped them away with a handkerchief she dished from her coat pocket. "His mail order bride had sent him a letter a few days ago warning him that her father was gravely ill and she was not going to go through with the marriage."

David's mother lifted her two fists in the air and shook them all around. "Oh, hallelujah! My prayers have been answered!"

"Sadie, if your prayers made this change then I say hallelujah, too!"

"David can marry you now." Sadie said it like it was already ordained.

She wanted to agree with the older woman but it was up to David. "Your son seems to think he is no good for anyone the way he is. I plan to change his mind."

Sadie stood. "I'll get my things. I'm coming along to help you."

After Sadie learned the doctor and Mabel were stuck outside of town, the two ladies spent the next hour gathering a bag for Sadie to spend the night there. "I'll put you in the room behind the kitchen. That's where Mabel used to stay. The steps will be too difficult for you to attempt to climb."

"That's fine, dear. I can help you with supper and we'll have a nice, entertaining evening to lift David's spirits. Stories of our lives in earlier times may help to make him realize how fortunate he is. We best be moving along."

It was a long trek back to the doc's office, especially since Sadie wasn't able to walk quickly. A few neighbors helped her along by shoveling a wider path on the side walk. Everyone in Belle seemed to care about each other. It was one of the reasons why Hope didn't ever want to leave.

She lifted her face to the clouds again, silently thanking her savior for the gratefulness in her life. She looked upon each day as a blessing now that she didn't feel forced to marry a man she didn't love.

She planned to walk down the aisle on Christmas Eve.

<> <>

"You brought my mother here?" He didn't sound too happy. "I'm fine. No need to make her come out in the cold!"

Hope was helping Sadie with her coat and hat when the older woman spoke up. "You let me decide about myself, young man! I'm here for the night, so get used to it."

Even though David sounded angry, when Hope stole a look as she hung up Sadie's coat, there was a warm grin on his face. He was happy to hear his mother's voice even though he tried hard not to show anyone.

She wanted to clap her hands in glee but restrained from doing so. After getting Sadie settled in the settee across from David, she busied herself in the kitchen, giving the two time to get acquainted. His mother's soft words seemed to soothe his soul. He was actually smiling at something she said when Hope came back out carrying a serving tray with centennial drops on a plate and filled-to-the-rim mugs of hot coffee. She set it down on the small table beside the settee and commenced to distribute the warm cups, along with a plate of cookies.

David's mother watched closely as Hope handed him a cup of coffee, taking both his hands and guiding his fingers. He lifted the cup by the handle with one hand while placing his other around the cup. She knew she had an audience and it made her slightly nervous, even though Hope had known Sadie since childhood.

This was different. His mother was soon going to be hers as well. As long as she was able to convince David.

"Tell me about Frank, dear. Has he gotten his medical degree yet?" The sly sound of Sadie's voice meant one thing. She was trying to induce some reaction from her son.

Hope sat down alongside his mother. "Frank was scheduled to come home this spring for a wedding. However, that won't happen now. I'll be marrying someone else."

"Who?" David's voice bellowed through the parlor.

The two ladies looked at each other and grinned. "That certainly got a reaction," Sadie leaned forward and whispered to Hope.

"I can hear you, Mother. Just because I'm blind doesn't mean my ears don't work!" His voice, filled with anger and frustration, lashed out at his own mother. When he realized how obnoxious he sounded, he frowned. "I'm sorry for speaking to you so, Mother."

Sadie tsked. "I accept your apology, son. Now, before you get too terribly excited again, Hope and I have an announcement to make."

He raised a brow. "An announcement?"

Sadie nodded. "Yes, son. Your best friend is going to have a wedding on Christmas Eve and we are going to help her."

"Hope?"

"Yes, son. Do you have anyone else as a best friend?"

He shook his head. "No."

Hope wanted to rescue him. His face fell and his shoulders drooped in defeat. This was not the reaction she had wanted. "Maybe we should let up on him, Sadie." She motioned to the older woman how distressed he looked.

Sadie shook her head. She knew her son better than anyone and kept at him. "Let me handle this," she spoke softly. She stood up, slowly making her way to her son.

She placed her hands on his shoulders and leaned over him. "Son, your father would be so proud of you today. If he were alive to see the good you have done in this town, he'd be the proudest man alive. Now, it's time you take stock of your situation and stop being so pigeon-livered, David."

His head lifted towards his mother. "I'm not afraid."

She placed a hand on his cheek. "Aren't you? Your father was a brave soul. He didn't want to go help that day on the mountain when those folks got caught in the avalanche, but he did. He had a feeling he might not come back. Yet, he went anyway. His courage and bravery never stopped him from being the kind of man he was made to be."

David huffed. "I know what you are doing, Mother. Where did it get my father? His courage got him dead."

Sadie kissed him on the cheek. "Your father is a hero. It gave a whole town the strength to save dozens of lives in that avalanche. One man's courage is all it took. Think about that for a moment before you judge."

David tilted his head as in thought before dropping his chin to his chest.

Sadie worked her way to the kitchen. "Let's see what we can round up for supper. Hope, can you give me a hand?"

Hope wanted to rush to David. He looked so lost and defeated. Sadie turned her head as Hope stood. The older woman shook her head. Hope walked past him even though it caused her great angst to do so. She almost reached out to him then took stock of the situation. David's mother knew how to handle him.

She hoped and prayed it would make a difference. Time was running out.

Chapter 8

David hung his head in shame. His mother had a way of making him see what was important in life. She didn't even have to say much at all. Her gentle hand on his face made him realize how much he cherished the woman who had always been there for him. Even when he had left home to find his own way, she was still a constant in his life.

She had a way of making him aware that life itself was a gift. He was blind. It hurt and he hated the fact he wasn't able to see. David knew there was no way to work as a sheriff again if he wasn't able to see. The best he could do was train the deputy to be the best sheriff for this town.

A knock on the door brought his deputy back inside, distracting him from his misery. Once again, the man standing in front of him swooshed his hands back and forth to warm his hands from the cold. "Don't you wear any gloves outside, Deputy?"

"It's cold out there, Sheriff. I stopped by to let you know that we have put together a team that's working on the tree right now. I've got three pairs of men sawing away. Pastor Elkins sent Miss Winkleman's class to the Belle Café to bring hot chocolate and sweets for the workers. We'll work as fast as we can, but I doubt it will done today."

"Thanks for the update."

He heard the deputy's sharp intake when David spoke cordially to him. The last time he had been hostile. He needed to make it up to the man.

"You're welcome, Sheriff."

"Deputy Will, my apologies for speaking so sharply before. When I am wrong I say I'm wrong."

"No need, Sheriff Knight. It can't be easy."

David didn't respond, even though his deputy was right. It was not easy to sit in a chair by the fireplace while every man in town was out helping to unblock a road. He should be out there with them. This is how his life was going to be for now. He had to accept things, plain and simple.

Even the fact Hope was getting married to someone on Christmas Eve.

He shook his head.

How did she find someone so fast? In less than a day? Why, she had just sent a telegram to Frank and now she was going to go off and marry someone else? It didn't make sense.

Then it did make sense.

He smiled.

"Are you all right, Sheriff?"

"I'm quite fine. If you go say hello to my mother, I believe you may be able to hornswoggle some centennial drops and a hot mug of coffee from her."

"Come on out here, Deputy!" His mother sure heard everything within earshot.

"I love those molasses cookies!" He left David sitting by himself in the parlor. David didn't mind one bit. His mind was working a thousand miles an hour, even faster than the fastest steam engine moved. Hope was planning on hornswoggling him to the altar.

He minded and yet he fell more in love with her.

David had been determined to keep her at arm's length and everyone else. Until his mother's words cut deep in his soul. A man was put on this earth to be of use to others. It didn't matter if they were afraid. His father had been afraid to go out in the storm. He had hesitated because he feared he'd never return back to his family. Yet, despite this fact, he didn't let fear hold him back.

Hope's sweet rose scent filled the air. She placed a hand on his shoulder. "Your deputy is having cookies with your mother. She is full of stories today. Would you like more coffee?"

"No, I'm fine." He reached up and placed his own hand over hers. "Will you do me a favor?"

"Of course." Her voice sounded hopeful.

He gave her a reassuring smile. "Is there a Bible close by?"

He felt her hand disappear from his shoulder, the loss apparent to his senses. He liked when she touched him to let him know she was right there. Although, he always knew when she entered a room. He smelled her sweet scent and knew where she stood when close by. There wasn't much a blind man didn't know.

"I'm holding the Bible in my hands. What do you want me to read aloud?"

"Second Timothy, chapter one, verse seven. Will you read that short passage to me?"

"Of course." He listened while the pages slid against the next one as she looked up the verse. "I believe for the spirit God gave us does not make us fearful, but gives us power, love and self-discipline."

"Thank you, Hope."

The book closed, its pages making a slight noise as she placed it on the table. "Is there anything else?" she asked, her voice low, yet wispy.

He slid front. "I'd like to rest awhile if you don't mind helping me back to bed."

"Of course." By the time she had him tucked in, David was so calm he knew it had to be a higher force affecting him. The passage she read he had heard all of his life. His father had always told him there was nothing a man had to fear if he had the love of God in his heart.

He had forgotten those well meaning words.

David had tried to live life on his terms.

It didn't work. Even if he had not been blinded by this accident, he knew there was a deeper meaning to life than how he had been living. He was accepting his fate. It was what happened and now he had to make the best of a bad situation.

God, if my sight never returns, help me to live the kind of life that will lift those around me up. Let me be a beam of inspiration and not wallow in self-pity. Amen and amen.

David's spirit was all right with the world. He drifted off to sleep knowing the love of his life was right beside him, tucking his blanket in, making sure he was taken care of. He wanted to tell her they would take care of each other. She had given him some medicine when he got in bed, causing his mind to get fuzzy again.

The moment he woke up, she was going to be the first person to hear how he had accepted his blindness and wanted to marry her no matter what.

<> <>

The rest of the afternoon flew by. Sadie worked with Hope at the stove to make some savory beef and vegetable soup that had the whole house smelling so delicious the deputy had asked to come back for supper. With a smile, he had also asked if he was allowed to bring a few guests.

"There's plenty for everyone," Sadie told him. "You tell the men out there we'll throw a few more vegetables in the pot so they can stop by for some hearty soup and oven fresh bread."

By supper time, there were eight extra mouths to feed in the doctor's house. The aroma of freshly baked bread permeated the air, while hands reached for the pot of churned butter to slather on.

David had woke up to the chaos. He seemed much more settled now that his mother was here. With Sadie around, there didn't seem to be a dull moment. She sat at the head of the table, politely conversing with each person as they supped, asking questions like a cordial host would do.

Hope had stayed in the background, secretly happy to watch while David chewed on his bread and nodded as the others talked. He even involved himself in the conversation and at one point threw back his head and laughed. She was afraid he would not allow anyone to see that he had to be helped to eat the soup.

That didn't happen. "Would you like some soup?" she offered. He nodded and accepted the spoonful, not seeming to mind that he had to have help in such a way in public.

Something had changed.

She felt it in the air.

Sadie had given her a wink and a smile. She had noticed, too.

As the night wore on, the others finished their meal, thanking the hostesses and leaving to go back to sawing for a few more hours.

"We all decided to work through the night in hopes the tree can be cleared up first thing in the morning." The deputy sounded quite proud of himself.

David grinned. "Fine job, Deputy Will."

"Thank you, Sheriff."

"Thank the men who are giving up their time to make this happen."

"Yes, sir."

The deputy was the last one to leave. Hope insisted Sadie sit with her son while she cleaned up the dishes.

"I'm here to help, dear. Why wouldn't I help you clean up?"

"I insist you go in the parlor and have some dessert with David. It isn't every day you get to be in his company."

"Which is quite wonderful, if you'd like my opinion!" His voice carried from the rocker where she had settled him in.

The two laughed. "I believe he's back to normal," Sadie teased. She gave Hope a hug and made her way to the settee once again.

Hope stood at the doorway, watching the two. She was one of the luckiest ladies in the world. Her mother-in-law-to-be was one of the sweetest, kindest women and her husband-to-be was one of a kind. But he didn't know he was going to be her husband, not yet.

Sadie happened to look up as her eyes lit up as if she remembered something. "I left a potato in the bin. Would you mind slicing it for me? I want to try an old remedy that I remember my own grandmother using for injuries."

Hope did as she was asked, knowing some of those old wives tales were just that, tales. What in the world was she going to do with a potato?

Twenty minutes later she found out. David was grumbling under his breath even though he knew there wasn't a thing he could do when his mother had something on her mind. "It won't take but a moment, son. Hold still."

Hope giggled as she took a slice of the potato and pushed it under David's cloth bandage. She moved it around until it seemed to fall right over his eyelids. "Mother, what in the world is that? It's cold!"

"It's a potato! Stop squirming!" She did the same to his other eye, pushing the slice up underneath his bandages again. He scrunched his nose and wiggled his eyebrows. Hope laughed out loud, wrapping her arms around herself, her shoulders shaking at the sight of the two of them.

"I'm not squirming. You want me to leave this over my eyes?"

"Yes. Do not touch them. I'll have Hope remove them in the morning. Now, promise me, son, you will leave them alone!"

He hesitated. Turned to where Hope sat watching. "Don't look at me, David. I can't help you against your mother."

Sadie nodded. "That's right, son. When there are two women in the same house, you may as well give up. You can't win."

"I'm starting to see that." He grinned. "Well, I can't see it. Not with my eyes."

Hope got up and gave him a hug. He wrapped an arm around her where she wasn't able to step back without being rude.

Sadie yawned and gave her son a hug. "I'm off to bed. I believe I've done my job here tonight. Hope, if you would not mind, I'd like to get home early in the morning as I have some of the ladies from the church stopping by at noon."

"Goodnight, Sadie. Thank you for all of your help."

Hope helped David back to his room, settling him in for the night. When she went to give him a dose of his medication, he held up a hand. "I think I'll be fine without it. I'm exhausted."

Surprised, Hope put it away and tucked him in. She gently gave him a kiss on his forehead. "I had a wonderful evening with you and your mother," she told him.

"I did, too. Thank you for bringing her. I know we are both tired this evening but there is something I'd like to speak with you about."

She placed a finger over his mouth. "Let's wait until daylight."

"Are you sure?"

"Yes. I'm certain. This has been an exhausting day, and a good day, too. I'd love for you to get your coat and hat on and step outside in the morning." She wanted him to keep moving along, so he'd want to enjoy life again and not be lying in bed all the time.

He nodded. "Okay. But, after that, we must talk."

Hope left his side, leaving the door ajar in case he tried to get up during the night. Her room was right at the top of the stairs, so she'd hear him if he tried to get out of bed and stumbled over something. So far he had been a good patient.

She slid under her covers and stared at the dark ceiling for quite a long time. Thinking about David's change of heart tonight was such a wonderful gift. She felt blessed and wondered what he had to say to her.

She closed her eyes, hoping it was what she had always dreamed about.

Chapter 9

A loud noise at the front door announcing the arrival of the owner of the house assured David the road was now open. Doc Robert's loud voice bellowed through the entryway. He knew exactly when Hope's footsteps came down the stairs and his mothers shuffled across the floor.

It didn't take long for Hope to open his door and stand by his side. "Good morning, David. I'm sure you heard the doctor is home. He's back and hearty as ever. I don't know what happened to him in that cabin he was hiding out in, but he has the widest smile on his face."

David chuckled and he knew when Mabel peeked her head inside the door. "How is our patient?" she asked, her voice no longer sounding grouchy.

"He's doing well, Mabel. I'm glad to have you back."

"It's a lovely day," she said before David recognized her steps fading away.

"She seems light hearted in her walk," he told Hope.

"I believe the two of them had a much needed vacation being holed up in a cabin with no way out."

David reached for her hand. He caught it in one try. Her warmth always made his heart race faster. "It may not be a bad idea."

Without his sight, he didn't know how she reacted to his words. Yet, he'd bet Hope was blushing. She tried to pull her hand away but he didn't let go until the doctor came bursting through the door. "Good morning, young man. How is our sheriff doing this bright and cheery day?"

"I'm still alive," David told him.

"I have every reason to believe you've been well taken care of by my wonderful nurse."

"She is amazing," he told the doctor.

"Yes, she is. Now, let's take a look at your eyes. Even though it's not time yet to remove your bandages, I'd like to get an idea of things." He turned to Hope. "I believe Sadie would like an escort home. I can take things from here."

"Certainly. I'll be back in a half hour."

When the front door closed, he sighed. How was he going to propose to her? Maybe he'd show up at the wedding ceremony and surprise her.

But, if all along her plans had been to get him to the altar, it would be no surprise. He chuckled to himself.

"You seem quite amused at yourself, Sheriff."

David leaned forward as the doctor unravelled the bandage. "I love her, doc. I always have."

Doc Roberts stilled. "I thought you had a young lady mail order bride ordered?"

"She isn't coming. Her father is deathly ill."

"I also heard Frank isn't coming back to marry our wonderful Hope."

"You did? How did you hear this?"

"McKready. You know how much of an early bird he is. He was actually helping the men to clear the path. He said you both were able to marry each other now."

"I'm not sure why he felt the notion to explain all that to you so early this morning."

Doc Roberts chuckled. "I asked him to keep an eye on things. He owed me a report. I forgave him his last ten dollars he owed me."

"He owed you money? For what?"

"He lost a bet." The doc's breath was too close. What was he doing? "David, why do you have potatoes on your eyeballs?"

He had forgotten about them. "My mother."

"You don't need to explain. Those remedies are fine for small wounds, but you've had quite a difficult time." He peeled the potatoes from David's eyes.

"It's been tough, Doc."

"Look here, son."

David turned to him. The doc was holding one of those magnifying glasses in one hand. He blinked several times and stared into David's eyes.

The doc was nodding.

David realized he was able to see the man clear as a bell.

His eyes widened.

He shook his head and blinked.

Blinked again. "Am I dreaming or awake, doc?"

A huge smile crossed the older man's face. "You're as awake as I am. This is good news."

"A day ago all I saw was shadows. I figured I'd be blinded for life."

"I didn't think you'd be able to keep that blindfold on there without looking once. It's why I said two weeks, but it looks like you'll be fine. Guess you'll be able to join us in the Christmas Eve ceremony this year."

It didn't seem like a half hour had passed, but he turned to look out the window to see Hope walking towards the doctor's office.

His heart sped up. She was the most beautiful sight he'd ever seen. "Doc?"

"What is it, son?"

"Do you mind if we keep this to ourselves for a few more days?"

"Why would you want to do that?" The doc turned when he heard footsteps on the porch. "Oh for Pete's sake, Sheriff! He leaned in, the old doc's eyes sparkling. "I found my own bit of heaven these past few days. Do what you have to, son."

Hope came in the room as the doc was winding the bandages around David's head. "How is he doing, doc?"

"His eyes are coming along as I suspected. I don't want to see him lying around here though. I think you can walk him around town, let him get some fresh air, also. Keep him busy so he can get back to normal."

David nodded. "I'd like to go to my office and sit there for awhile, if you don't mind taking me, Hope?"

"Not at all. I knew sooner or later you'd be up and about. Congratulations, David. You are progressing."

The doc turned back to the two of them. Even though David wasn't able to see through the bandages, his senses were still heightened. "I think the more time you keep him from this bed and get him moving, it will improve him and enable him to get back to normal. I suspect in a few days his eyesight will return to normal."

Hope clapped her hands. "That's wonderful news. Did you hear what he said, David?" She leaned over and gave him a hug. "I told you not to lose faith."

David wrapped an arm around her and pulled her closer. He felt like a fraud but at the same time he wanted to surprise her. He had an idea in mind.

She was going to have the best wedding a woman like Hope deserved.

<> <>

"BUNDLE UP. HERE, LET me get those." Hope tsked, tsked like a mother hen while she buttoned David's jacket. He was standing by the door, allowing her to help him dress to go outside. His cap and gloves were secured, along with a winter scarf that looked oddly familiar. She wiped imaginary dust from his collar. "There you are, all ready."

The wind had settled down some so when she opened the door it didn't take them by surprise. She was glad it would be calm for David's first venture outside. "Brr, it's quite chilly," David told her. He moved closer. She helped him from the porch and they were on their way up the street towards the sheriff's office.

"Well, good afternoon, Sheriff Knight. It's good to see you out and about."

"Hello, Livvy. Has your husband let you leave your store?" Livvy and her husband owned the mercantile.

"Well, I told him I was going to see the sheriff come back to life. I'm glad you are feeling much better."

"I'm the reason you left your four walls? I'm honored." David took a slight bow and gave her one of the biggest smiles Hope had seen since he got hurt.

"Good day, Sheriff. Miss Hope."

Several other townsfolk waved and patted the sheriff on the back, happy to see him out.

"Oh, no! Here comes Lucy!"

The sheriff stopped in his tracks. "It's best to get this over with or she will follow us to my office. I can't have her there all day long."

For ten minutes Lucy filled him in on what was happened all over Belle from the stranger who disappeared on the day David was hurt to what Ruth Winslow was making for supper at the boarding house.

"Thank you for doing your civic duty Lucy, but we have serious business to attend to now. Can you do me a big favor and have Paps stop in to see me as soon as possible?"

Lucy nodded and walked down the street so fast if Hope blinked she'd think the woman disappeared into thin air. "That was excellent, David. Now I know why you are sheriff of this town. You know exactly how to handle that woman."

He grinned. "I do now, don't I? I believe we are at my office."

"How can you tell?"

"I can smell the aroma of delicious food at the Belle Café."

"Turn here," she told him, guiding him up the three steps to his office door. "Deputy Will is already here. Won't he be surprised to see you?"

He was indeed surprised and happy to see the sheriff. Helping David into his chair, he gave Hope a hug and thanked her for getting him out.

"I'm going to go back and help the doctor with some patients. David, I'll leave you here for an hour and a half. Would you like to eat at the café later today?"

"Let's see how I feel when you come back," he told her. The two lawmen were so engaged in a conversation, neither noticed when she slipped through the door. Hope gazed in through the window and smiled.

Everything would be all right.

She gave one last look up to the sky, thanking her God silently for how far the man she loved had come.

Now all she had to do was get him to the altar Christmas Eve.

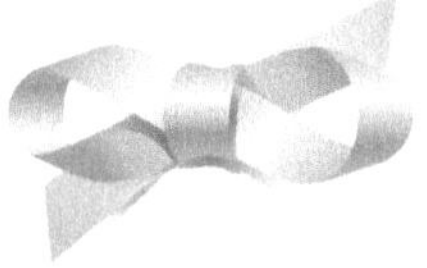

Chapter 10

"Is she gone?"

"Who? Hope?" Deputy Will sat down on the chair in front of his desk, directly facing him.

"Yes."

"Is there anyone else here?"

"Who else would be here?"

"No one in the jail cell?"

Deputy Will laughed. "Of course not. I haven't had the pleasure of arresting anyone yet since you've been out."

"I need your help."

"Sure, what can I do?"

"There's a wedding I need to arrange."

"You? What the heck? Isn't that kind of stuff left for the women to do?"

"Now, Deputy, this is the modern age. Men help make arrangements, too. Especially when they want to surprise someone."

"Who do you want to surprise?"

David grinned. "I think you already know the answer."

"Hope. Are you planning a secret wedding to Hope? Does she want to marry you? Have you asked her?"

"Stop with the questions! Of course she wants to marry me. I also have a secret I want you to stay quiet about."

"There he is! The man on that horse we thought had the bells! Sheriff, I can't believe this!"

David stood. "Don't do anything foolish, Will. Stay calm. Keep your firearm in its holster. What is the stranger doing?"

David feared he'd have to pull the bandages off. He would if he needed to because the towns safety came first. For now, he'd let the deputy handle this. A tiny fear tugged at his throat. Last time the deputy handled a crisis, it almost killed him.

"He is coming in here."

"Let him come in."

The door to the office had a bell that made a faint jingling noise whenever someone came through. It alerted David to pay attention. He sat back down.

"Good afternoon. I'm looking for the sheriff?"

"I'm Sheriff Knight. This is Deputy Will. What can I do for you, stranger?"

"I hope I'm not going to be a stranger for long. I bought the old Kemper place across the creek a few weeks ago. Name's Bartholomew Kendleton. I'm a friend of Sebastian, the trapper."

"That's funny, we never heard of you before now." Deputy Will was acting awful brave even if David heard the slight fear in his voice.

"It's because I came here a little over a week ago and something spooked my horse. She was out of control and I didn't get a chance to come back until now. The road was closed from the tree."

It all made sense. Sebastian and David would have lunch at the café when he came down from the mountain on occasion. The trapper often talked about men he met. The name Bartholomew rang a slight bell. "Speaking of bells, we heard them when you were getting on your horse."

The man opened his jacket and produced a small rag doll. Around it's neck were two bells. David had since pulled the bandages up along his forehead so he could look at the man. He seemed sincere.

Bartholomew gave it a shake. The tiny bells jingled quite loudly. A sadness shadowed the man's face. "It's soon Christmas and I wanted to give this to someone who needed it more than me. It's been sitting in my saddlebag for over a year now."

David saw the sorrow in the man's eyes. Something terrible had happened. "Who did it belong to?" he asked, trying to keep his voice steady and low. He didn't want to spook the man.

Deputy Will opened his mouth when he noticed David had the bandage off his eyes. David put up a hand and shook his head slightly.

"My daughter, Clarabelle. She died almost a year ago. Her mother is gone as well."

The room was silent for so long, David worried the man would turn tail and leave before he had a chance to speak. "I believe Charity has a daughter who would love the doll. She works in the café. I believe she's there now."

The tall man with the sad face nodded. He was pretty choked up. "I just want it to go to someone who'll love it as much as my Clarabelle did."

With those words, he nodded to the men, turned and left. Light jingles from the doll rang through the office, almost like the bells they had been looking for.

"That settles things then. Jeez, Sheriff, here comes Hope."

"Don't say a word about my eyes. I want to surprise her at our wedding. I'll speak with you about it after we come back from lunch."

The two put their heads together, talking softly in monotones while Hope pointed out the way to the café for the stranger.

<><>

"There is something going on. What were you and Deputy Will whispering about when I came in?"

She sat across from David in the Belle Café, enjoying a bowl of soup. David was in such a happy mood, she hated to ask but there was something in the air she wasn't able to put her finger on.

"I don't know, Hope. I was discussing the business of law if you want all the boring details."

"Then why did you stop when I entered?" she accused. "I know you too well, David. You tried to cover it up by changing the subject, but did you know you clench your teeth when you don't want to talk about something?"

He grinned. "I never knew I did that. Are you sure?"

"I'm as positive as I'll ever be." Her attention went to the stranger who stood by the counter while Charity gave him a hug. He seemed taken back by the simple gesture.

"What are you watching?" David asked, the bandages secured around his eyes.

"How do you know I am watching something?"

"I hear the change in direction of your voice. Your beautiful voice."

She blushed. He was forever complimenting her. "That's about the sixth time you've told me I'm beautiful today."

"Because it's true."

"David, please. What's gotten into you?"

"I'm happy to be alive and well."

"The doc says your eyesight will return in a few days. Just in time for the Christmas Eve celebrations. I'm so glad."

"I don't want you to worry if it doesn't happen. I'm okay with everything now. My mother made me realize how fortunate I am, Hope. A man does his best and better if he knows how."

She patted him on the hand. He held her hand, intertwining his fingers with her own. "I'm glad you are my best friend, Hope. I wish I was able to do something wonderful for you."

"You can be my partner for the Christmas Eve celebrations. After all, it was supposed to be your wedding day."

He frowned. She thought that was odd. "Why the sad look?"

He shrugged. "I don't know. Hope, it is going to be so hectic and busy on Christmas Eve with all the ceremonies planned and the big celebration later. Do you realize how many couples are getting married then?"

She did know. "Quite a few."

"I don't want our friendship to ever fall short. So I'd like to take you out for a special night the night before Christmas Eve. I'd like for you to have all the attention."

"That is so sweet, David. But, the doc isn't going to remove your bandages until the day before Christmas."

"I don't care. I don't need my sight."

Hope was shocked. She gave him a squeeze. "What a powerful statement, David. I'm glad you've seen that it's more important for people to be together and love each other than it is to worry about a few tiny things."

He laughed. "Hope, eyesight is a pretty big thing."

She lightened up. "You are right. I'm proud of you, David."

"You told me that. How about it, will you? The evening before Christmas eve? I'll wear my fanciest suit and you wear your prettiest dress and we will walk out together."

"Walk out? Are you asking to court me, David?"

He gave her one of those handsome smiles she loved. "Something like that."

She sighed. "Either you are asking me or you are not!"

"Then I guess I am."

"Okay."

"Okay."

The two left the café, strolling along the boarded walk until she dropped him off at the sheriff's office for a few more hours. She turned back to wave but he had already gone out of sight.

Mabel fixed her hair and helped her put on a beautiful coat she had given Hope. "It was my daughters's coat. Now, it's yours to keep. Look how nice it fits you."

"Thank you." Mabel's daughter had passed on a few years ago. She was hired by the doctor soon after and moved in to be his housekeeper. Now, it appeared that she was much more than that, Hope realized. She wondered if they'd ever marry. The two of them had been spending a lot of time together in the parlor.

A loud knock sounded at the front door.

Mabel and Hope went to answer at the same time to find McKready standing there.

Hope's face fell. She thought it was David. "Oh, hello."

McKready's eyes sparkled. "David asked me to escort you to the church. He has someone he wants you to meet. He also invited the Doctor and Mabel."

"Oh?" She turned to find the two putting their winter coats and hats on as if they had planned to go out all along.

Disappointment ran through her like a snowball rolling up a hill. She had thought David wanted to court her, but this wasn't courting. Not with a whole crowd of others. McKready held out his arm when she stepped outside.

She took it, a frown forming on her mouth. Walking across the street, the others laughed and talked about the ceremony tomorrow. Hope didn't have too much to say. She had been looking forward to spending the evening with David. She even went out of her way to wear her best dress.

"It will be fine. David has a surprise for you, Hope. Don't worry."

She raised her chin in the air. "I'm not worried."

He chuckled, waving to a few others who caught up and followed them.

By the time they were at the front door of the church, a small crowd had gathered. Hope turned. "What in the world is going on? McKready? You can't hide things well. Now, tell me what David is up to?"

"That would ruin the surprise." He pulled open the front door of the church to find more townsfolk sitting in the wooden pews.

Hope looked around. At the end of the rows, standing near the pulpit, was David. He wore his best Sunday suit with a white button down shirt, fancied up right down to a pair of shiny shoes.

Then she looked into his eyes.

His eyes!

The bandages were no longer covering his face.

She gave him a warm smile.

Then, she threw back her head and laughed out loud.

David did the same.

Music began to play softly in the background. The pianist played slowly as Hope marched to the center of the room where she began her trek down the aisle.

Her smile never wavered. She closed her eyes and almost ran into one of the wooden pews until McKready pulled her back. It wasn't easy walking with eyes closed. She couldn't imagine what David had gone through these past few weeks. "How long has he had his sight?"

" A few days. The morning the doc got back."

"I should be angry," she told him.

"He wanted to surprise you and give you the best gift ever."

"He did."

"Tell him. He looks awful worried."

"Maybe I'll make him worry a tad more. That was pure trickery."

"It was. Make him squirm. I'd like to see that."

McKready and Hope shared a knowing look as he handed her over to the man who was about to become her husband.

"Hope." David took her hand in his, slowly bringing her hand to his mouth. He pressed it against her and held it there.

"David."

He looked into her eyes. "You are my best friend, Hope. I've loved you since I've known you. I can't imagine spending my life with anyone else but you. I'm sorry I didn't realize it before and left here to find something out in the world. What I was looking for was always right here. You."

A tear slid down her face and she didn't try to swipe it away. "That is the most beautiful thing anyone has ever said to me."

"I'm not worthy of you and I'm selfish at times. I've gotten blessed with getting my sight back. I now know you'd stick by my side no matter what. If I'd be blind right now, you would still be here. I've come to realize you are the woman I love. Hope, will you marry me? Right now, today?"

She was so emotional there were no words. She didn't want to agree without saying something but the words were stuck in her throat. "I will," she gasped. He gathered her in his arms.

Hope heard the congregation let out big bursts of air. Everyone had been holding their breath. Someone called out and another person began to clap.

Pastor Elkins smiled, but his frustration showed when he had to raise his hands and call out to restore order. "Ladies and gentleman, shall we have a wedding today?"

The crowd cheered. Hope wasn't really paying attention. She was staring into David's clear brown eyes, mesmerized by their clarity and the depth of his love for her that she saw in them. "I love you, David."

"I love you, Hope. I'll always love you."

Their lips met and the congregation clapped.

They both laughed when they heard the town gossip in the front pew. "That sheriff has always been a bit rambunctious. That ruffian is kissing her like that before he's supposed to!"

One of the older townsfolk called out. "Quiet down front. I haven't had this much enjoyment in years."

Hope and Dave gave each other a long, loving look before turning to the pastor, who was patiently waiting, a curve to his mouth and his Bible opened. "Shall we begin?"

"Yes."

"Yes."

<><><><><>

• • ❧ • •

Thank you for reading *A Tin Star for Christmas*.

Frank Mason, the man who went to Philadelphia, has some explaining to do.
Read his story next:
A doctor wanting redemption - A disbelieving woman - Can she take him at his word?
Mercy Lane has always loved Frank, even though he was engaged to someone else. Then, he leaves for medical school and breaks the engagement. She doesn't ever expect to see him again since he claims he wants to be a big city doctor.
Now, he's back to proclaim his love for Mercy. How can she believe him?
Frank Mason came home to Belle to ask forgiveness for his prior behavior. There is another reason: Mercy. She is the reason he isn't able to go through with a marriage to someone else. He had always loved her even when circumstances made it impossible. Now, he wants to make things right and tell the woman he loves the truth.
Can he be redeemed?

． ． ∾ɸ∽ ． ．

OR
Would you like to read all 3 of the stories I've written for this series in one shot? Get the binge-worthy boxed set on Amazon today!
Get Cyndi's Belles of Wyoming Boxed Set on Amazon[1]
(https://www.amazon.com/gp/product/B08XPS4W26/)

---

1. https://www.amazon.com/gp/product/B08XPS4W26/

Cyndi's Books

Mail Order Brides of Wichita Falls Series

Ruby
Grace
Lily
Charity
Hannah
Rebecca
Sophie
Ellie
Jenna
Leila
Boxed Set Vol 1
Boxed Set Vol 2
Christmas in Wichita Falls Holiday Book

Brides of Mill Ridge Series

An Outlaws Honor
A Reverend's Rose
The Ranger's Redemption
A Doctor's Devotion
A Teacher's Treasure
A Sister's Sanctuary
Brides of Mill Ridge Boxed Set

Sons of Nora White Series

A Bride for Luke
A Bride for Adam
A Bride for Samuel
A Groom for Nora
A Bride for Russell
A Bride for Wesley
A Groom for Widow Young
Sons of Nora White Boxed Set Volume 1-4

Multi-Author Series Contributions

A Bride for Abel - The Proxy Brides series
A Bride for Arthur - The Proxy Brides series
A Tin Star for Christmas - The Belles of Wyoming

Candy Cane Christmas - Ornamental Matchmaker Book #10
A Bride for Calvin - The Proxy Brides
Viola - Angel Creek Christmas Brides
Dallas - Bachelors & Babies series

Contemporary Small Town Romance

Florida Keys Romance in Paradise Series

The Tomorrow Serial
The Forever Serial
Escape Serial
Island Keeper
No Name Inn Series
Boot Key Harbor Short Story Boxed Set
Santa's Wrong Turn & Save Me Santa Holiday Shorts

All these books can be found by visiting https://www.amazon.com/Cyndi-Raye/e/B00ENA1WEG

FREE Chapter - A Bride for Abel

Chapter 1

.. ✤ ..

"Nuts!"

Jim Grover stared at his opponent, his head wobbling slightly. "I give you my word if I lose this hand, you can have my horse and wagon. But I am a betting man and I think I can win. What more do you want?"

Abel Roosevelt stared back through the white and gray smoke filtering through the the Silver Spur saloon. Noise from other patrons in the back ground didn't rattle him. As a matter of fact, he was pretty good at filtering out any distractions. Abel knew how to focus on one subject. Like the man in front of him who was about to lose a card game fair and square.

He spoke in a clear, calm voice. "You know the rules. If you're going to make a bet like you just did, you need to bring the nuts from your wagon wheel and throw them into the pot." Abel wasn't going to mess around long with this fellow. He was too drunk for his own good.

"That's only for men who will take off if they lose a game. I stick to my word. A man's word ain't good enough for you?"

"That's not what I said."

He guffawed. "It sounds like it to me!" The drunk shifted, taking another slug of the rot-gut whiskey.

Abel didn't drink. He always liked to keep a clear head no matter where he found himself. He had the upper hand in this case, but he wasn't going to take the man's belongings. He had come in here to grab a bite to eat and play a game of cards, maybe win a few coins. He should get up and walk away. Except, that wasn't his style. Abel liked to see things through, good or bad. Staring down at his hand, he knew the hand he held was hard to beat.

"Let's finish the game," he told the others, wanting to get back to Miss Sue's Boarding House and call it a night.

There had been four players at the table over an hour ago. One man threw in his cards and was long gone. The man beside Abel threw in his hand. "I'm out," he told the two. "Spent my allowance and I ain't stupid or drunk enough to gamble my horse!" He nodded to Abel and stood, staring hard at the drunk. "Jim, you best get on home, too. Hang it up before this stranger rides your new horse and wagon right out of town!"

"Mind your own business," Jim barked at him. His eyes were nearly closed. He swayed once or twice but then seemed to come to life after another shot of whiskey. "Let's get on with it, then. I don't plan to lose tonight."

The other man shook his head. "You say that every week, Jim."

Abel was tired and getting annoyed. "We can stop right here, friend. I don't want nor do I need your horse and wagon. You can keep your belongings if you fold right now."

That seemed to infuriate Jim. He pushed back the wobbly chair, almost dropping the bottle. His pudgy stomach prevented the bottle from tipping over and falling to the floor. Jim grabbed the neck with his fist and raised the bottle, dripping whiskey down his chin. He swiped his hand across his mouth. "You plan to keep all the money in the pot?"

"I was ahead until you offered to place another bet with your horse and wagon since you're all out of cash. If you stop now, we can each walk away. You keep your horse and wagon, I'll keep what I've won. If you insist on finishing the game, I'm afraid you may lose it all."

Jim Grover slammed his fist on the wooden table, drawing the attention of several men standing at the dark wooden bar. The sounds of jaw-jacking were silenced with the bump of a hard fist. "I ain't never quit a card game, *friend!*" he spit out, raising his voice until all eyes were on him.

I see how you're going to play it. Don't go for your gun. Abel looked as calm and serene as a grandmother knitting on her front porch. Inside, he was watching every single move Jim Grover made from the twitch of his right eye to the jerk of a left cheek. He studied the man for several moments under hooded lids, deciding if the man would go for his gun or let dead dogs lie.

Even the music came to a halt as the piano man ceased to play. He was a burly sort, his belly round and a jolly looking face that was no longer smiling. "Do we need to get the sheriff?" his husky voice called out to the barkeep. Abel didn't turn around to let the man know a sheriff wouldn't be needed. He was going to talk Jim Grover into heading on home.

He hoped. It was hard to read a drunk.

A few glasses clinked as the barkeep stood behind the counter with both hands in the wash water. Abel doubted he was washing dishes. Most likely the barkeep was fisting a pistol as tension build up in the air.

Abel came to the conclusion if the man wanted to finish the game then it was his own dumb luck when he lost. He didn't like to take advantage of others, but men in a drunken state were too unreasonable. Abel nodded to the drunk. "What'll it be then? Play or walk away?"

"Play."

"Then get your nuts."

The dark look the drunk gave him had Abel on edge. The eyes that stared him down were troubling. Jim Grover teetered on the balls of his feet, then turned as if in submission and made his way outside.

"Maybe we'll get lucky and Jim will pass out before he gets those nuts off the wheel. He's getting worse every time he shows his face in here," the barkeep spoke up, not really saying it to any particular person.

Abel tended to agree, except he never lived on luck.

After twenty more minutes passed, Abel decided it was time to end the night. "I'll be heading out," he told the barkeep. "If the man comes back, you tell him we parted ways fair and square."

"Will do, mister. Don't you worry none, Jim won't remember what happened once he sobers up."

Abel gathered the money in the pot and threw the barkeep a few coins.

Someone shouted from outside.

"Jim Grover! Put that away! I said right now! I won't warn you again!"

"Sounds like the sheriff," the barkeep announced.

Abel didn't want to run into the law tonight. He had enough dealings with them in his job as a bounty hunter. Sometimes they got along with him, other times not so much. He didn't care to find out if this one was friendly or not.

The bat wing doors flew open with a bang. Jim Grover stood there, his chest heaving like a wild man as he pointed a shotgun directly at Abel.

Disgust seeped into Abel's veins. His fingers lowered to his hip as he met the threat head on. With a quick flick of his wrist, his gun was pointed at the drunk. Abel watched with guarded eyes as the man didn't hesitate but began to squeeze the trigger.

Abel was faster. The next thing he knew Jim Grover was on the floor of the dusty saloon, face down as his shotgun clattered to the ground. Abel had thrown himself out of the way when the shotgun blast went off. He leaned into his fall, winding up on one knee, still holding on to his own smoking weapon.

His sixth sense made him realize someone was right behind him. Abel turned to feel his skull connect with a hard object. Almost instantaneously, he noticed the barkeep hovering over him and a man with a silver badge walking towards him before total blackness.

<> <>

Abel moaned. His head hurt like nobody's business. Lifting a hand, he felt for any sign of an open wound. His eyes popped open when he found a lump the size of a goose egg on the back of his skull.

A chair scrapped against the floor. Footsteps got louder.

Where in tarnation was he?

Abel turned his head to find steel bars keeping him from going anywhere soon. He groaned as he sat up. "What am I doing in jail?"

A man appeared in front of him on the other side of the cell. Abel tried to blink to clear his head but to no avail. No sense in trying to stand, he mused. There wasn't anywhere to go in the small locked cell. He noticed the five-point star on the tall man's shirt front. It was the same man who stood before him when he was knocked down in the saloon. He was older with a head of black hair. Spots of gray streaks dotted his short cropped hair along with a well-trimmed beard.

"Looks like you got some serious problems at hand, mister."

Abel closed his eyes. No sense trying to pretend to see with the double vision he was sporting. "What's my crime, sheriff?"

"Since you killed a man in cold blood I'd say that's enough reason."

Able shot up, moving to the cell door in front of his accuser. "He had a shotgun aimed dead at me. I saw him pull the trigger."

The sheriff smirked. He shook his head and frowned. "Now, mister, I don't know what you saw, but everyone in the saloon agrees when that poor drunk Jim Grover came through the door you took a shot at him and killed him dead."

"That's not true." He was trying to stay calm. "I aimed for the shotgun. There's no way I'd kill a man dead if I shot his trigger finger."

"I got news for you, mister. He's being buried as we speak. You must be a bad aim."

"I'm an excellent aim, sheriff." This wasn't going down well. The sheriff was avoiding looking him in the eye. Most liars did.

Either way, Abel stared, unrelenting. "What do you want from me, sheriff?"

"Name's Sheriff Nelson."

Abel waited.

The sheriff took his good old time, pacing back and forth in front of his desk with both hands behind his back. After a few minutes of dead silence, he figured the sheriff would realize he wasn't going to panic.

Sheriff Nelson turned and sat on the edge of his desk. "What are you doing in my town?"

"Just passing through."

"That a fact?"

Abel nodded.

"What do you call yourself?" Sheriff Nelson stared at his hand, picking at his nail like he was having a casual conversation.

"Abel Roosevelt."

Sheriff Nelson pushed away from the desk. "We have a serious problem here, Mr. Roosevelt."

"We sure do. You got the wrong man in jail."

"I tend to disagree. Take a look outside."

Abel didn't have to look out the large dirt stained window to see a noose hanging over a large sign at the Blacksmith shop. It was put there for his benefit. The sheriff was trying to scare him. It was working. No man wanted to die at the end of a rope.

He looked at the sheriff as calmly as he was able to. The man wasn't going to see him sweat. "What do you want?" he repeated.

"Well, I'll tell you, Mr. Roosevelt. Since you done killed my niece's groom, she's out a potential husband. That don't sit well with me or my sister in Pennsylvania."

"I didn't kill the man. There is no way I hit him with a fatal shot." Abel had been a sharp shooter in the war. He knew how to hit his target no matter how much pressure he was under. Although, he doubted he was going to be able to convince the sheriff.

"I say different. I'm the law in Pistol Ridge. No one knows who you are. You can argue all you want, but the fact is the townsfolk will believe me. So will a Judge."

Abel knew he was right. Most newly sprung up mining towns didn't have a strong justice system except for vigilantes and crooked sheriffs. Once in a rare while an honest man stood behind the badge.

Abel sat back down on the rickety hard bench. For the past four years he had found work as a bounty hunter. He'd brought in some hardened criminals and never shot a man who didn't deserve to be dead. Most of the law and order he saw was crooked. No one would really care if he lived or died.

He was weary.

It had been a good run.

He guessed it was time to meet his maker.

"I have a proposition for you."

Abel closed his eyes, no longer interested in the sheriff's games. "I'm not doing your dirty work, if that's what you want out of me. If it's my time, then I guess it is."

He didn't budge from the spot when the sheriff began to grumble about men with pride. When he heard the man's heavy breathing, Abel lifted one eyelid to find the sheriff standing in front of his cell. "Here's the problem and you are going to fix it or hang. My sister died and her daughter is in need of a husband. My niece is having a child out of wedlock and she needs to marry. We had it all set up for her to marry Jim Grover by proxy."

"I don't see it as my problem."

"Mister, aren't you tired of chasing the wind? Going from town to town not settling down?"

"You don't know what I'm tired of. Hang me, sheriff, if you can prove I am guilty." Abel didn't want to hang, but he wasn't going to let the sheriff know.

The older man scratched his jaw as if he just thought of something. Abel had a feeling he knew exactly what his next words were going to be. "If you stand in for Jim and marry Kate, I'll sign over Jim Grover's farm to you. He gave me the deed to hold for some money he owed me."

Abel didn't doubt it was a gambling debt. The dead man was in over his head. He almost grinned at that thought. Except it wasn't funny since he was the one sitting here in jail.

"I'm expecting my niece on the stage next week so there's no time to waste. It's either marry her by proxy or hang." Sheriff Nelson took his hat from the hook by the door. He turned. "You think about it for awhile. When I come back, I'll take your answer."

Abel figured he'd get one shot at this.

Marry a woman with a child on the way, and in exchange he'd get a farm.

Or, hang.

Any fool would take the latter. Giving up his freedom wasn't all that difficult. It had been a long four years of working all over the countryside hunting down men he'd never want to know. Abel didn't know much about farming, but he guessed he'd learn.

But, a wife? He had some thinking to do. He turned his head to see the sheriff across the street. The man deliberately turned towards the jail and took a firm grip on the noose. He swung it back and forth, staring hard at the glass window. Abel glared at him through the bars even though he knew the old man wasn't able to see him.

The door opened and a tiny woman entered. She held something in her hand. "Hello? Mister, are you awake?"

Her small voice carried to his cell. "I'm awake."

She shuffled across the floor. "I brought you some supper." Her sweet smile had Abel up and reaching for the plate in a flash.

"Thank you, ma'am."

"Oh, gosh. Don't call me ma'am. Everyone calls me Miss Sue. I was expecting you back at the boarding house, and when you didn't show up I had to rent out your room. I'm sorry to see you in jail."

Abel grunted while he shovelled food in his mouth. It was so good. She mashed the potatoes into a creamy mix and the roasted meat melted in his mouth. "Me, too."

She leaned against the steel bars. "Psst, just in case you are wondering, rumor has it that Mr. Grover was up to his ears in financial debt from gambling."

Abel nodded. "I figured so."

"Well, I also heard through the rumor mill that he owed the sheriff big time. He even handed him his deed to his farm."

"I already know that part, Miss Sue. Sheriff already disclosed that bit of information."

"Humph. Well, did you know there is speculation that you didn't shoot the man dead? It was the sheriff that did."

Abel stopped chewing his food. He tilted his head to take a look at Miss Sue. Since she owned the boarding house, she probably heard a lot of talk. "How many know this?"

She huffed. "Why, almost everyone. I make sure to let everyone know what's going on in Pistol Ridge. It is my duty to do so."

The town busy-body. Abel usually steered clear of women like her but not today. Today he was actually happy to talk to her. "The sheriff wants me to stand in for Jim Grover and marry his niece by proxy."

"Well, of course he does!"

Abel scraped his plate clean and handed it back to her. "Why do you say that?"

Miss Sue turned to look out the window to make sure the sheriff was still across the street. He had disappeared. She crept across the floor and looked out the window. "He just stepped inside Glick's Telegraph office. I'll find out from Earlene what he sent out."

Abel frowned. "Is there anything that happens in this town you don't know about?"

Miss Sue gave a wide smile. "Hardly anything. Mister, you have some time before he comes back, but if I were you, I'd take him up on his offer. Otherwise, you'll be swinging before breakfast tomorrow morning. They'll take matters in their own hands and won't wait for the judge to come through."

"I doubt I can prove it. The sheriff seems determined to make me a husband for his niece."

Miss Sue scooted close to the cell. She reached in her pocket and pulled out a few cookies wrapped in cloth. "Here. These were baked this morning. I'll tell you one more thing. Old Doc Malburn, is sweet on Miss Walters who owns Betty's Bonnets, and she told me this morning the doc said Jim Grover was shot in the back."

Abel suspected the fatal shot hadn't come from his six-shooter. Now, he knew for sure. "Why are you telling me this?"

She leaned in as close as possible, her nose and mouth so close to the steel bars. "The whole town knows the sheriff is dirty, except for those three lackeys he calls deputies. No one will stand up to him. He does bad things here and most people are afraid. Maybe you should take the offer and then high-tail it out of here as fast as you can go."

Abel had the same thought. If only he was a man who ran from his problems. "I was offered the Grover farm if I marry his niece."

"Well, you better figure out what it is you want to do. Because, if you don't do what he wants, you will hang."

"I don't want to hang."

"Then get out of jail and help us run this sheriff out of town. We all figured you as the most likely to do so, the little we've seen and heard of you."

"You were talking about me already?"

"The whole town talks, mister. We need a hero here. You're the most likely one we've seen in awhile."

"I'm no hero." He was in jail, behind steel bars. A hero didn't wind up in jail the same day he rode into town. He sighed. It would be nice to settle down somewhere and rest his soul for awhile. "Did you ever meet this niece of his?"

Miss Sue stepped back. "No, never. But I heard she is homely and that her aunt where she resides wants her out." Then she leaned in closer again, looking back and forth. "Earlene, Mr. Glick's wife, said her husband has been sending and receiving telegrams for the last week. His sister, not the other one that died but the other one, doesn't like Kate because she was left an inheritance they want.

Whatever steps they are taking, it is for the sole purpose of taking her money from her."

"The sheriff said she was with child."

"I don't know anything about that, but if she is, then she needs a husband. And, since you don't want to hang, it all makes sense to use the proxy marriage as a way to get out of jail. You can investigate the sheriff from the farm."

A Bride for Abel is live on Amazon![1] (https://amzn.to/2Nrt1Yh)

. . ❧ . .

. . ❧ . .

.

---

1. https://amzn.to/2Nrt1Yh

Don't miss out!

Visit the website below and you can sign up to receive emails whenever Cyndi Raye publishes a new book. There's no charge and no obligation.

https://books2read.com/r/B-A-PXQ-GHTDC

BOOKS 2 READ

Connecting independent readers to independent writers.